R.F.D.
Journal

by BILL KNIGHT

Mayfly Productions

A Mayfly Production

Cover photo: Jack Bradley
Cover art: Ralph Hubbard

The author gratefully acknowledges the publications or broadcast programs in which some of this material first appeared: WMBD-AM 1470, Illinois Public Radio Network, Peoria Journal Star, POP magazine, Pekin Daily Times, Heartland Journal, Springfield State Journal Register, Illinois Publisher, Oil! magazine and The Labor Paper.

ISBN 0-9624613-2-6

Manufactured in the United States of America.

Special thanks to WMBD-AM's Greg Batton, Jim Clasing and Lindsay Davis; WIUM-FM's Bill Wheelhouse and Don Johnson; and Shari Royer of The Labor Paper and Peoria Typographical Union/CWA Local 29.

For Terry.

Additional copies of this book are available for $5.99 plus $2 postage and handling per order (not per book) from Mayfly Productions, P.O. Box 513, Elmwood, IL 61529. For bulk discount or other information, please write.

Table of Contents

48,063

Introduction

A Patti Smith song says: "People have the power to dream, to rule, to wrestle the world from fools."

"Well," you say, "that's a nice sentiment, but it can't be done."

Not so! Look around in your own neighborhood or town. You'll find people acting on that dream.

R.F.D. Journal presents some of these folks, folks who show an indomitable spirit and hearty insight facing floods and poverty but also facing the passing of everyday work and time and life.

Most Americans have a lot of faith and ideals and gumption. Of course, Will Rogers said, "We can't all be heroes, because someone has to sit on the curb and clap as they go by." But my heroes are not sports stars or five-star generals who get parades. I think America's real heroes are ordinary people willing to make a fuss to make a difference, ordinary people doing extraordinary things, quietly and steadily giving of themselves to make our country a better place.

A couple of years back, I asked a farmer what he thought of Congress' trying to maintain the status quo in agriculture policy.

"Hightower," he said, " 'Status quo' is Latin for 'The mess we're in.' "

Well, he's right about that, and that's why I admire the spunkiness of people I meet out in the countryside. They're figuring out new ways to do things... making sense and making progress.

Jim Hightower
Nationally syndicated radio commentator

Photo by Linda Henson

Jim Olt, third-generation duck caller.

Places

News judgment and appreciation of the "ordinary" was explained in this passage, where journalist Christopher Scanlan quotes philosopher Will Durant: "Civilization is a stream with banks. The stream is sometimes filled with blood from people killing, stealing, shouting and doing the things that historians and journalists usually record; while on the banks, unnoticed, people build homes, make love, raise children, sing songs, write poetry and even whittle statues. The story of civilization is the story of what happens on the banks."

--Press Cuttings

Traveling from Little America to Wilbern, Wyatt Earp's Monmouth birthplace to the Ranchhouse in Bureau, a rural-route Schwan's man to a small-town vet, stories happen here. Here are some others.

The call of the wild game

(SOUTH PEKIN)-- The sound is neither brass nor beast. A bleat? Almost. It's not fish; it's fowl.

Each hunting season -- and all weeks between-- calls of the wild still echo from a small complex of outbuildings behind a two-story white frame house outside town here. A stand of shade trees towers above the lot, where the railroad tracks pass by a sign that reads "P.S. Olt. Game and Bird Calls."

"We manufacture calls for a great many species of birds," says Jim Olt, the 54-year-old company owner, "ducks, geese, turkeys, pheasant, crows... gosh, partridges, quails, even hawks, although people don't hunt them."

Olt literally grew up around the business. Thumbing through a full-color, 16-page company catalog offering merchandise from instruction records to decoy anchor cords, Jim stresses that it's the hand-made calls-- and some instincts and appreciation-- that've kept the Olt family in business for 89 years.

"The calls are hand-tuned, which means each one has to be individually put together and blown by someone who knows what it's supposed to sound like," Jim says. "After they hear it, they can file it or otherwise adjust it until it's right.

"You don't get a degree in 'game calls'," he continues. "We have experts, hunters, but it's still a process to learn the sounds, and you learn, you acquire personal knowledge, by being around something."

Olt himself has been around the business for decades, learning not only the nuances of bird calls, but the other calls also made and sold here-- coyote and fox, bobcat and elk. He-- and the firm-- have grown considerably.

"The company started in 1904, and I'm the third generation here," he says. "We started the company and the family's been involved in it ever since.

"Now we sell to distributors and catalogs, certain chains and direct to some dealers."

Olt's shop is busy with a handful of employees finishing fill-in orders to ship to sellers anxious to serve their customers. They sell "triple raspy diaphragm" turkey calls for less than five bucks, and a gift-box package of duck and goose calls that lists for $75.95.

Relatively small, the operation specializes. And it's world famous.

"We've just preferred to keep the business ourselves," Jim says. "We've had offers to sell by various specialists-- and generalists-- in the sporting goods industry who want to get into it. There's a tremendous amount of competition.

"But, like I say, we want to hang on to it," he says, pausing for effect. "I guess the Olts have a high threshhold for pain and disappointment."

He laughs.

Although occasionally tempted by such offers to sell-- or to relocate-- Olt resists, exploiting the opportunities right here in central Illinois.

"It's probably an advantage, overall," Jim says. "Certainly, we're centrally located in a national sense, so that transportation is relatively convenient. But there's more, too. In a small area like this, a small company like ours can operate efficiently, yet also not sacrifice its character."

Amid all of the business challenges and even... artistic challenges-- workers and users have to learn to "play" the hand-made calls just like musicians on new instruments-- Olt tries to pick out the best part of his work.

"I've grown up with it, but I still like being around hunting and hunters," Jim says. "The outdoors is sort of a fringe benefit, I guess-- although you can't always hunt when you want to if you're busy at work.

"And besides the people and the activity, there's a certain sense of pride with doing a job well."

Behind us in an adjoining room, there's a squawk. After a moment of silence, the noise becomes more of a sound. It blares again.

"Canada Goose," Jim says, smiling.

'Julmarknad' says it all

(BISHOP HILL)-- Marking the time when a few wise men followed a star to a Bethlehem manger, Christmastime crosses cultures to celebrate... light, and optimism. And good.

At Bishop Hill northwest of Peoria, the good people are stringing lights and hanging pine boughs and having a holiday marketplace tied to their Swedish heritage.

"Julmarknad," says Judy Anderson. "Jul is Christmas in Swedish and marknad is just the market. What it amounts to is Christmas market."

Judy, a 51-year-old shopkeeper here, concedes that the local artisans working throughout town, the free old-fashioned horse-drawn wagon rides, the walking "crea-

9

tures" from Scandinavian folk myths, the music and the baked goods and children's programs all... help business.

"A lot of it is that the shop owners have gotten together to make the Christmas Market to get people to come to see what Bishop Hill is all about," she says.

However, Anderson-- a lifelong area resident whose own roots can be traced to Sweden, where she's visited-- knows there's more than commercial appeal. There's a sense of history. And hope.

"I think the decorations and also the St. Lucia Nights are real neat to see," she says. "You drive into town and see all these lights in all these windows."

A colony of Jansenites more than a century ago pioneered this place in the Henry County flatland. Bishop Hill now has about 200 residents and a designation as a state historic site. There are beautifully restored brick-and-stone buildings and a pretty little white gazebo in the village square park.

But there's also a ballfield where the bakery and brewery stood in the 1800s. And places, pleasant enough, sell antiques and so-called country crafts and gifts. Times have changed since the Christian settlers came and went. But this season, there's a special... glow here.

"We like to get people to come here to understand Bishop Hill, and why Bishop Hill is here," Judy says. "This is the only area that these people came. There were no other Jansenites in any part of the country, so we are unique.

"We get a lot of people from the Chicago area," she continues. "In fact, we have probably a lot of people in a 50-mile radius who've never been to Bishop Hill."

And after Julmarknad are Lucia nights, when more light and music and... idealism are planned.

"All of the people coming to Bishop Hill, they all come in with smiling faces and they all just seem to be happy to be here, and they're not like every other shopper who's out there growling, 'I gotta pay this' or 'I gotta spend my money.'

"Here they always have this smile on their faces."

Onion rings of truth

(DODDSVILLE)-- For 15 years, the members of three village churches here have decreased to fewer than 30, a number that now relies on lay preachers, a solid sense of humor and a special money-making venture.

"Doddsville is just a small, rural community that sits on the McDonough County-Schuyler County line, and there are just two or three houses there," says Marshall Litchfield, a 53-year-old activist with the Doddsville United Methodist Church-- which serves parishioners who formerly attended all three local churches.

"Not so many years ago, that was a trading center in that area, but when the highway went through in 1926, that's when the small towns and the small railroads began to falter. Since that time small towns have begun to dwindle," he continues. "So, Doddsville's down to just a small, country church, but there's a group of people there that are special people and good friends and they like to worship in that church, in that close, community atmosphere and togetherness that's involved there.

"We think the small church really is something of value," Marshall says. "It's interesting. People come to our small church to worship and say, 'Boy, I come from a big church, but I really appreciate the closeness and the warmth of the small church.'

"Of course, we look at the big church and we're envious of their programming and think, 'Boy, if we had all those Sunday school classes and all of those things...,' so there's kind of both sides of it."

Just east of Route 67, Litchfield farms, a job and a way of life that might strengthen his tolerance and his appreciation for religion-- and the fellowship he and his wife, Joyce, enjoy in their little church.

"All of our denominations, you know, were based on the same Bible and the same set of beliefs and the same principles," he says. "Although sometimes we think we're so much different, we're still pretty much the same."

"There's the chemistry of the people there," he says about the Doddsville church. "I think it's just a special, friendly group of people and that's the key element there. Again, as far as the spirituality with your church-- whether it remains a spiritual church or just turns into a social club-- that hinges on your people as well as your leadership."

There's a casual warmth in the Litchfield home that probably connects with their congregation, a determined lot that pitches in.

"The financial end of it works because our lay people are not paid anywhere near what a full-time person is," Marshall says. "And we've been doing some fund raisers that help our budget a whole lot."

One big fundraiser has become a Labor Day tradition, as the Doddsville folks are featured at the annual Antique Gas Engine Show and Flea Market at Argyle State Park near Macomb. For the last three years these church people have made and sold TONS of onion rings. Literally.

"A few years back, a few guys at church had been on the Spoon River Drive and they came back one weekend and said, 'Onion rings is the thing. We watched on Spoon River Drive and people eat onions'," Marshall remembers. "So one thing led to another.

"We started with one fryer and that first year tried to slice the onions ahead of time at the Industry Methodist Church, and had everybody about half sick and the church smelling bad-- a real mess. But this group doesn't give up easy, so we decided an assembly line process might work the next time. People peeled, sliced, put them in the mixture, and fried them and gave them to the people. Since that time, we've just improved and expanded.

"From that one fryer, we've now got six fryers mounted on a trailer, along with our serving tables," he says. "Then we've got a tent that's 16 by 40 feet that we set up over the top of that."

Again, Litchfield reminds us, once work gets under way, squabbles seem minor, if not petty. And priorities return. Like peddling 2,000 pounds of onions. Like fun. And faith.

"You know, we get together maybe for a worship service and we have a little trouble communicating," Marshall says. "But when you work together, elbow to elbow, why we communicate a little better than in a worship situation.

"I think sometimes people look at our churches and think that it's such a stuffy situation that nobody's supposed to laugh or have any fun there," he continues. "But church groups can be fun groups, and this particular group, I think maybe that that's one of the drawing points, really, that Doddsville has."

Fishin' (It's not the fish)

(GOODFIELD)-- The sign is visible but small. Insignificant. It reads: "No trespassing".

No one acknowledges it, standing around by this bend in the Mackinaw River in southern Woodford County. People are just fishin'.

"I've been fishin' since I was a little kid," says Robin Ratton, hoisting gear out of the side of her hatchback.

Parked off the hard road, the car contains several poles and tackle boxes, three kids and two adults, and... baskets full of the enthusiasm and arcane wisdom of veterans who've fished all over the country, who see the Illinois River and area strip-mine ponds and tributary streams and local lakes as subtly different.

And absolutely identical.

"We've got two or three poles set up differently here," Robin says. "My daughter wants to top fish, for bass, so we've got her set up for that. My son likes to catfish, so we've got the heavy weight to set him on the bottom. And it's different in the river than in the lake, because a river will have the current pulling on it, too.

"Fishing the rivers and stuff is all basically the same."

Ratton, 33, last spring moved to central Illinois from central California. She recognizes drought; she doesn't miss the smog.

"Blue skies are great!" Robin says. "We've been out to Eureka Lake and got a couple of catfish, but we haven't been fishin' in about two weeks. We have noticed that the water is down everywhere. A few weeks ago here, you couldn't walk around the bend, and today there's a big sandbar. But we don't know what effect it's going to have on the fishin' yet.

"We haven't seen as much problem here along the Mackinaw as we did when we'd fish the San Joaquin in California, where there's a lot of foam and stuff built up along the sides. Here, it's been pretty clear.

"But, now, we went fishin' with my cousin while we were down in Arkansas, and the water there is a lot clearer than it is here. You could fill up a glass jar and see no sediment. It was clear, clean water, where here it's green and yucky, so it's just a difference everywhere."

Wearing a purple hooded sweatshirt, Ratton reflects on the ultimate delight of fishin'.

And it's not the fish.

"Once you get the kids put in the water and kind of settle down, I just like to sit and relax," Robin says. "Be outside, in the fresh air.

"It's always better when you catch fish. But, you know, you have a good time whether you do or not."

Maurie's: more than apples

(PEKIN)-- In the windows of the three-storefront, yellow-brick building in the 500 block of Court Street here, yellow-and-black cardboard boxes are displayed, saying: "Maurie's Popcorn. Seasoned to your taste. It's always popper fresh."

It's special; it's obvious.

"Popcorn, the cheese corn, the caramel corn-- y' know, you don't get that everywhere, not like you get here," says Jean Beeney, an employee at Maurie's Book-A-Rama. "And his caramel apples are real famous. But I'm not real sure what we're going to do this year, though. We'll see how it goes."

Jean Beeney at Maurie's.

As Beeney explains Maurie's and its wares, its neon signs outside seem to crackle with cool colors, like autumn's trees' leaves, like... chilly temperatures.

Like Maurie Smith's legendary caramel apples.

"Every fall," Jean cites the apples' old schedule. "We didn't have any last year, 'cause he passed away in August. I don't know what the daughter's going to do this year. It's still up in the air.

"Once you start those apples, you got to have them everyday," she continues, laughing, "cause people can get real nasty. It's a real popular item.

"They've been calling, now, for the last month about those apples," she says. "They call from all around. Those apples have gone so far around. People ship them. They're just hot!"

There are very few places like Maurie's left-- places with several counters for candies, with out-of-town newspapers and paperbacks and cigars. Maurie's keeps going for its public, Beeney says.

"We have loyal customers, and I think the help here is friendly and we're kind of like family here. That has a lot to do with it. We all work as a group. We try to be nice to our customers, and we have customers who keep coming back-- every day. We have a lot of people come in and out of here."

Part of the attraction is the sweet smell, too, she concedes.

"It's his special recipe, that caramel," Jean says. "Not everybody knows how to do that. That was his own thing."

Between the lines-- in her eyes-- Beeney, 58, reveals that much of Maurie's recipe was for more than caramel or candy. He had the secret ingredient for business. For busy-ness.

"I think our busiest time is Valentine's Day," Jean says. "Valentine's Day around here-- you just wouldn't believe it. People are lined up in here, like... well, like--"

Jean's voice trails off, and she acknowledges that the workers here miss Maurie. But they take refuge in his "recipe": togetherness.

Does working as a team help?

"I feel like it does, yeah," Jean says. "A lot of us have been here a long time-- a few of us have been here a LONG time. So we just all continued on. He was a great person, Maurie was, and we all felt like he was like a Dad to us; if we had a problem, he had a problem. After he was gone, we all sort of hung together for his memory. We hung in there. We do just like we did when he was here."

And as far as the caramel apples-- it's still unclear, if not undecided, whether they'll be back.

"Once you start it," Jean explains, "then you've got to continue. Maurie would do this for maybe a month, then that was it for the year. If we start it, then we'll continue; if not, we'll maybe let it fade away. Let the memory be there, but if we can't keep it up, just let it go with him."

Floral philanthropy

(GRANVILLE)-- Most plants just need a drop in their buckets to thrive, says florist and philanthropist Nick Van Wingerden, fingering one of many drip irrigation tubes that wind through a 20-acre indoor growing facility on Route 89 south of town.

Since he learned that, Van Wingerden has tried to help young seedlings. And old people.

Folks from North-Central Illinois to Eastern Europe have benefited from his family's life-long dedication to plants and people.

"I feel like I was born in a greenhouse," says Nick, the 40-year-old Christian who runs Mid-America Growers. "I'll probably die in a greenhouse."

Nick tries to practice, not preach, his faith, he says.

"We have a quiet lifestyle and a good business, both based on Scriptural principles," Nick says. "It seems to work well. We're at peace."

Established in 1971, this wholesale-only operation employs about 250 people in the spring, when it does about 60 percent of its annual business. Mid-America produces almost 400 different plants for gardens, hanging baskets and pots, and ships almost 400,000 poinsettia plants nationwide to buyers such as K mart and Sears.

Their reach has grown since Nick's father, a former truck driver in the Netherlands, moved here after World War II. Aart and Cornelia Van Wingerden successfully combined their love of the Earth and a Dutch instinct for plants with fertile opportunities here, Nick says.

"The whole family is in the business," says Nick, the father of five and the eighth child among a brood of 12 brothers and four sisters. "We each found our own niches."

To help meet the rather fickle U.S. market, which mostly revolves around holidays, Van Wingerden says he constantly changes the huge indoor complex here.

"We take breakthroughs from other nations and customize them to North America. We continually modernize," Nick says. "We expanded in '91 and again this year. We have to keep expanding."

The complex is made of several connected buildings that will total more than a million square feet. Environmental conditions are completely computer-controlled: temperatures, light, moisture, and humidity are all maintained with space-age precision, Van Wingerden says.

Workers with walkie-talkies drive electric carts down eight-foot-wide paths linking growing areas. Whooshing by banks of boilers that heat the facility, they carry wagonloads of cardboard boxes of plants. Roofs are covered with a double layer of plastic instead of glass, saving construction, energy and repair costs. Ceilings reveal lines of water pipes for heat or for nourishment. The gravel-and-concrete floor is cluttered with thin hoses.

"Some of my growers are like artists," Nick says. "It's like they know what plants are thinking, when they need more heat or fertilizer. I'm more businesss oriented. That helps me know we have to always improve or we'll lose it."

The Van Wingerden clan isn't exactly losing it. However, some might say that they're giving it away; others that the family firm is gaining. Growing.

Nick and three of his brothers have a low-key humanitarian project Van Wingerden makes sound simple.

"We have a duty to the desperate, the destitute," Nick says. "There's no way people should tolerate starving people, homeless people. This is no big deal; it's just our responsibility as citizens who are able to help."

Past Van Wingerden projects have helped poor people in the Caribbean and Indonesia, in Rumania and Africa. One, at a small village in Mali, brought water wells and irrigation, agriculture and education.

Seeing televised news reports about the Ethiopian famine in the mid-'80s inspired the effort, Van Wingerden recalls.

"I saw pictures from there and it made me sick that this could be happening. So we got involved," Nick says. "We just happen to have the skills, the energy and the money to help. We hooked up with a mission agency because we have the resources but not much time, and they have the time but not enough assistance."

So, from water and seeds to blankets and knowledge,

the Van Wingerdens are giving. Developments they helped bring to the Mali village included a generator, a cistern, and a modified drip-irrigation system in a field that's now yielding vegetables.

"There's a 50-acre farm where there used to be just sand," Nick says. "For 50 families, things are happening. It might be happening at a snail's pace, but it's happening. Eventually, we hope they'll grow more than they need, so they can be self-supporting and start selling their excess and then paying a percentage of their crop into a fund to create a new project. And that one could grow. All this could happen even if we quit, or die."

That's a little like immortality, a visitor comments.

"No, no no. We're just trying to be a drop in the bucket," he says. "When we face the Lord, I hope He'll consider us some small asset to our community and country and the world-- not a liability."

Gale's signs of spring

(CANTON)-- There are traditional signs of spring: the arrivals of breathless robins and lamb-or-lion winds; the sprouting of spindly violets and hearty morel mushrooms; the timeless quality of a day that's escaped from an icy prison.

But here in Fulton County, spring can come, too, with the ordinary and eternal signs of change and life and love found all around. Like at Gale's Lounge.

"Business really picks up in the spring," says Gale Derenzy, the 55-year-old owner of the tavern at 68 E. Elm. "People start to get out a bit more, and the retirees who've gone south for the winter are back in town and back in here."

When Gale's starts to welcome back its regulars, sell more chili dogs, pull more drafts of Pabst and let baseball dominate afternoon television, all those mundane yet meaningful acts are accompanied by slight, subtle changes. And different lives.

A couple of springs ago, patrons accustomed to the sameness of Gale's long-time location at 71 E. Elm had to get used to its new site when Derenzy bought the building across the street.

"We brought everything with us," Gale says. "A couple of pieces of the back bar broke and didn't make it, but everything else-- the bar, the fixtures, the signs... heck, the people."

And the atmosphere.

Despite all of the world's whirlwind changes-- despite even time's inexorable progression from summer into fall, then to winter and spring-- Gale's for decades has seemed to age with dignity, with a comfortable lack of change inside its doors. In fact, different times show on different clocks here. There's also rich mahogany and other polished wood, old electric signs and hand-lettered reminders that harken back to different eras, back to other times of tradition, kindness, warmth and protection from progress' indifferent advances.

Four years ago here, the late Jim Johnson-- who died this summer-- mused about Gale's Lounge.

"Gale's is a refuge," said Jim, a retired truck driver. "I've been a regular here for 30 years, I'd say, and it's always been a comfortable place to go. It's a great place to just stop in and visit. There's no jukebox and the TV's on only for news or sports, so you can hear each other talk."

Johnson had looked up at a televised Cubs-Dodgers game and sighed. His weathered face wrinkled a bit as he grinned.

"A guy can bring in his grandma or wife and not feel out of place," he'd said, smiling.

His wife, Irene, seated at his elbow at the curve of the long bar, had laughed and adjusted her Cubs cap and started teasing Jim like a schoolgirl flirting with a backyard athlete.

"I won't knock down another guy's team," she'd said, her happy eyes squinting at the familiar family feud she was fueling, "(but) the Cardinals are going to be shot down anyway. They're funny enough without a joke."

Jim's white moustache had seemed to twitch and he fingered his own (Cardinals) cap and gestured toward a Cubs wall calendar with a game schedule.

"You know what 'S.D.' stands for?" he'd asked, pointing to an upcoming Padres-Cubs series. "South Dakota. The Cubs might stand a chance against South Dakota."

Irene had laughed and leaned forward from one of the stools.

"I admit it; I'm weird," she'd said. "But it's not because I'm a Cubs fan."

The day bartender, Donnie Bowler, had lighted an unfiltered Lucky Strike and smirked. Quiet and courteous, Donnie'd strolled past the tidy shelves of sparkling clean glasses and shiny bottles and served up chili dogs and Andeker beer to a couple of new faces.

The chili dogs here are classics, with grated onions and sweet relish daubed over a frankfurter covered with a tangy meat sauce. Emerging from the steamer, the franks perspire and the buns seem as soft and sweet as cotton candy.

Gale's has been in Canton under one name or another since the repeal of Prohibition. First, it was a gambling parlor, then a typical American neighborhood tap and now a friendly, family-oriented tavern-- maybe a low-budget sports bar. (If so, of course, Gale's was a sports bar long before some marketing flack made up the term "Yuppie", much less before Yuppie businessmen created the male-bonding alternative to fern bars.)

"When I bought the place in 1985, I cleaned it up a bit, but I wanted to keep it special," says Gale, a former Pabst beer distributor and Canton school board member. "I cater to the family and younger adults, who might bring in their kids for hot dogs. I want to maintain that atmosphere."

There's a large sign near the cash register-- "Absolutely no profanity allowed"-- yet a blue-collar ambience remains, perhaps outliving those many years long past when workers from International Harvester and Caterpillar, from area mines and farms, all filed in and filled up the place for after-work drinks.

An old woman in a print dress sits at one of the red vinyl-covered chairs at one of the five tables and sips a soft drink while waiting for her own chili-dog lunch. A couple of chrome coat racks have caps and jackets hanging limply in one corner. A few plastic imitation Tiffany lamps with beer-label logos sway slightly.

Irene had beamed when Ryne Sandberg hit a home run off Los Angeles that afternoon a few years ago, before Jim died. She clapped and laughed and ordered a round of beers as customers watched the TV replay.

Echoes remain from the excited conversations then, conversations that accompanied a couple of visitors' exit from the pleasantly dark bar outside into the sunlight bathing downtown Canton.

Through the changes in storefronts and in the lives and memories of and about its regular customers, Gale's Lounge has aged well-- like Scotch whiskey, Cuban tobacco or Louisville Slugger wood.

Like a clear, 75-degree day in spring.

Supremely cheesy

(SPARLAND)-- Ambience is a term too quickly tossed off these days. Before Baby Boomer, cedar-scented fern bars grabbed the word, ambience meant atmosphere, or flavor. It's a word whose meaning is as lost as that of other words, like loyalty and stability.

"I've given the owners about 17 years, off and on, since '68," says Barbara Wilkins. "It's not a full-time job; I only put in four hours a day, about 28 hours a week. But I like it. I like people."

Wilkins, 60, stands behind the counter at the Supreme House of Cheese here, and she welcomes a lone visitor fleeing the ground fog to stop in and sample its charms.

"This has always been like this since they bought it in '68 or '69, I think. It's always been like this."

"This" is the kind of place that schoolkids and truckers,

farmers and retired housewives, all feel at home. A block east of Route 29 on Ferry Street, the Supreme House of Cheese has a handful of tables and chairs in its entryway, and a big, high-ceilinged main room filled with roomy racks and shelves of chips and candy, gloves and paper goods, dairy products and trinkets.

"It's a general store, but business is very slow," she says. "The holidays are pretty good, with cheese trays and party trays for people. And then we have truckers stop in; we make up sandwiches and we try to give them a hot soup every day.

"We make our homemade doughnuts and rolls every morning, so they come and have coffee and doughnuts, and drop back at noon for a sandwich and a bowl of soup."

Tall porcelain cases contain cylinders of cheeses and meats. Peering through glass, a customer points to the colby or bleu or cheddar or American. It's not fancy, but it's pretty fine. And it's convenient.

"Our regular hours are five in the morning 'til seven at night," Barbara says. "We close at six on Saturday, and Sunday we're open 'til maybe 3:30 or 4 o'clock. Open at six. We're open seven days a week; we really only close two days a year, Christmas and Easter."

Tonight, traffic is slow. Or easy. Or lazy. There's no rush. There's no gas or video or bank machine, just friendliness. And sometimes that's all you need-- along with a carton of milk and some baloney.

Wilkins smiles slightly and touches her collar, displaying a modest, reserved air. And poise. And pride.

"We have people come up from Peoria, who've bought cheese here and they come back," Barbara says. "But all our customers, they're glad that we're here."

Say it right: San Jose

(SAN JOSE)-- A sign in the storefront next to the Country Companies Insurance and real estate office in San

Jose reads "For sale or lease."

It's a Sunday afternoon, and the churches and schools are as vacant as the streets winding beneath the water tower and the grain elevator, past the veterans memorial and the bank, by the auto body shop and auction house. It's quiet.

" 'Bout the only thing open today, now, would be Casey's up there on the highway," says Bill Hayden, 66, a Town Board trustee here. "The Standard Oil station used to open on Sundays, but they said they didn't have the trade. Now three other fellas took over and they decided they wouldn't open on Sunday either, because they run from Monday through Saturday from six to six, so all the employees there just have one day off now."

A lifelong area resident, Hayden recalls busier times.

"Oh my gosh, when we used to have trains going through ever so often and with the elevators, it was pretty busy at one time. We used to have a big cheese plant right out here, and we had a big seed-corn drying plant that was here. It's all gone now. Back when I was 18 or 20 years old, it was pretty busy. Had a big hardware story here where the bank is now. It's all gone now; it's really quieted down since I was a young boy."

We're in the town building two blocks south of Route 136, a block from the Logan-Mason County line, which splits the village. Hayden is standing near a short strand of small Christmas lights, lying on the floor by a meeting table cluttered with calculators.

"I'm trying to put the Christmas tree lights up today," Bill says, laughing. "I got 'em scattered out on the floor in there now, trying to get them lined down."

Although San Jose may not have a lot of activity, it does have an identity-- its name.

"A lot of people said you should never call it 'San Hosay'," he says. "There was a fellow by the name of San Jose-- with a 'J' sound-- that started it. This is what I've always heard. People around don't like to have San 'Hosay' said, 'cause that's in California. We like to have it here said San 'Jose' just like it's spelled."

Chuckling, Hayden says the town's relaxed pace is a

plus for the residents here, who like the laid-back atmosphere. They like it enough that San Jose has stopped losing people, he says.

"It's kind of stable. It seems like people come down, especially in the summer, because it's easy living for summer use," Bill says. "A lot of times in the winter, they move out again. We have an awful turnover as far as water stuff-- my wife takes care of the water stuff-- because people are leaving and coming in all of the time. You never know who's where unless you keep good track of them.

"But overall, you know, the same population is pretty much here that's been here for years. Now and then there are new faces, though."

Leaving town, a visitor drives past Styninger's beautiful brick funeral parlor and sees a civil defense siren rusting out back behind the Farmers Inn Restaurant.

Peaceful.

Old-fashioned business

(HANNA CITY)-- A modern marketing consultant might be amazed at Meyer's Discount, on Route 116 here. They don't really promote their products or services, or plan much merchandising. But there might be method to their madness. Or... messiness.

"We don't do any advertising. It's just word-of-mouth," says June Fletcher, a three-year employee at Meyer's, where she's standing behind the counter at the cash register, surrounded by a pleasant-- homey-- clutter. "People talk about the store and its products and prices. We do a big business in men's jeans and hunting clothes, for example. People come in from all over-- Chicago, Iowa, we have a regular from Missouri who stops in every few months. He called today and said he was coming by to buy socks!"

Socks are certainly here, on and under shelves also

Photo by Linda Henson

June Fletcher at Meyer's.

crammed with dry goods and food, toys and tobacco, housewares and hardware.

"It is pretty unique here. Different," says June, 60. "If they look, customers can find almost anything here because, well, it's just a little bit of everything, really.

"If something's on the market, sooner or later we'll have it," she adds. "Almost everything has been here at one time or another."

But one wonders: Does it take long to figure out where everything is? (Where ANYTHING is?)

"Not too long, really, because when you work with the merchandise you pick it up pretty fast. We put it away and keep an inventory upstairs," she says, tapping her head.

It's been some time since the Meyer family opened up and became a local... well, fixture, for folks of all ages in the area, Fletcher says.

"The store's been here between 25 and 30 years," June says. "The town restaurant might be kind of the local meeting place, but we're the only store in town, really, so we get steady traffic.

"And it gets real busy when the kids get off the bus," she continues. "They stop in for snacks-- chips and so forth."

Meyers' penny candy and 99-cent rack do brisk business, she adds.

"We sell a tremendous amount of novelties," she says. "It's hard to keep it filled some weeks. I mean it."

Amid all the malls and national chains, conventional wisdom would be that such increased competition could threaten such places. Not, so, Fletcher says.

"It hasn't bothered us at all-- and some people don't believe that," June says. "It's unbelievable, isn't it Brenda?"

Brenda, another clerk, looks up and nods, and June-- a petite brunette-- smiles and suddenly seems to savor the... anarchic approach to buying and selling.

"It just happens here. We're nothing fancy," she says, laughing. "People enjoy rummaging around, I think, so they come in and browse and eventually they find something they were after-- or something they just stumbled across."

Outside, black tape almost covers a broken sign that

used to promote the Illinois Lottery. A red Yamaha scooter is parked on the sidewalk not far from a one-ton Dodge flatbed truck. A trash barrel holding cardboard boxes stands on steps near five pop machines and a pay phone. Being old-fashioned works, it seems.

"It definitely does here," June says. "Sometimes we'll have a case lot of something and somebody'll come in the next day and it'll be gone. I mean it, it's unbelievable."

'MIGHTY Mississippi'

(NIOTA)-- It's mid-summer, mid-afternoon, and some of the dozens of prisoners volunteering at Niota along the flood-wracked Mississippi River are filing through the Dallas Rural Fire District garage, where women from local churches are ladling a pleasant-smelling casserole onto paper plates. Lynn Ford, a local gun dealer, is supervising this makeshift operation, one made efficient, he says, by those very volunteers.

"Oh, like the Salvation Army and things like this," Lynn replies when asked who's helping. "Church groups have helped us, a lot of private businesses, things of this nature. We have correctional facility people in here and they've been a tremendous help. They furnished us with anywhere from 75 to 125 people a day. It's worked out real good for us. They've done a super job. If it hadn't been for their cooperation and help, we wouldn't be here right now."

Ford, 49, has been out here before on parts of the three-mile levee protecting this century-old, working-class village of 143 people from the river, swollen by a summer rainfall twice as wet as last year's.

From Gumbo Flats in Chesterfield, Mo., to the Warsaw Bottoms south of Hamilton, Ill., rivers ran roughshod over banks, levees, towns and lives. Around Quincy, Ill., routes 24 and 61 divided the damaged from the salvaged. On one side are fields with tall corn and deeply green beans; across

During a 1985 flood of the Illinois River, Tom Harms rowed home to his Rome, Ill., residence with supplies: two 12-packs of beer.

the hard road are acres of brown crops and dying fish.

The National Weather Service says the Flood of the Century started on June 8, when the Minnesota River flooded Jordan, Minn., and a storm settled over much of the Midwest, showering between three and five inches of rain on the region in a few hours.

Months later, the statistics are staggering. Throughout nine states, more than $6.5 billion in crops over 23 million acres are lost. The hardest-hit land totals some 54,000 square miles, an area roughly twice the size of Lake Michigan. Another $4 billion in property damage is estimated, resulting in 74,000 people evacuated, 46,000 homes damaged or lost, and 45 people killed.

The flood, which breached more than 800 levees, destroyed much of the so-called infrastructure of mid-America: hundreds of bridges hurt-- including every bridge between St. Louis and Kansas City-- and thousands of roads; hundreds of small towns evacuated and thousands of farms vanished under water. Many domesticated animals abandoned; wildlife in disarray.

In Illinois itself, four flood-related deaths were reported, along with estimates of $930 million in property damage and $600 million in agricultural losses. There were 9,000 jobs lost, and 34 counties receiving disaster aid. It's a bona fide disaster area, according to state and federal officials.

U.S. Agriculture Secretary Mike Espy, who visited the battered region 12 times, said the flood was the worst in 140 years. After Congress passed a $5.7 billion relief bill, Espy said, "We know more money will be necessary, and I'm sure the members of Congress will receive a supplementary request."

But the emotional toll has no pricetag, and the deepest scars may happen on this, the smallest scale.

"What do you say to someone who has lost their home, their business and everything they own?" asked Donna Harris, a Dallas City preacher talking to reporters. "Some of them can't even come to church because they don't want people to see them crying. I can't sleep nights thinking about it."

In Niota, there's a black Labrador retriever wading and swimming east of the white-washed cinderblock firehouse. There are dishes of water and pet food on roofs for other stranded, panicked cats and dogs. Some people are inside, filling and tying bags. Others-- young and old, men and women, black and white-- are outside. Crowded along the highway-- itself below the nearby water level-- some shuttle sandbags to the adjacent Santa Fe Railroad bed, and others stack them in an orderly but desperate action.

"The main part of the system is on the river itself, along the river," Lynn says. "What we've mainly done is build them up higher to hold more water. We're keeping the leaks plugged that spring out. Keeping them reinforced."

Ford -- looking around Niota's flood-relief headquarters and adjusting his wire-framed glasses, then his NRA baseball cap, then a pen stuck in the pocket of his blue work shirt -- is reluctantly prepared for the worst, he says.

"We don't know how long the high water's going to stay with us," Lynn says. "As far as cleanup, we have a flood control committee, and we kinda take care of the cleanup."

'93 Flood Relief

Organizations assisting the disaster area:

American Red Cross
Disaster Relief Fund
P.O. Box 37243
Washington, DC 20013

Salvation Army
Disaster Relief
P.O. Box 1621
Des Moines, IA 50306

Farm Aid
P.O. Box 228
Champaign, IL 61824

World Relief
The National Association of Evangelicals
P.O. Box WRC
Wheaton, IL 60189

Catholic Charities USA
Midwest Flood Relief
13331 Pennsylvania Ave.
Hagerstown, MD 21742

B'nai B'rith Disaster Relief Fund
Midwest Relief
1640 Rhode Island Ave., NW
Washington, DC 20036

Cleanup will take months and many forms throughout the region. Here and there, only rows of grain bins sticking up from the muddy brown water demonstrate that there's more beneath the flood than the brush and timber barely visible above the surface. In Hardin, Mo., the Missouri River swept through the graveyard and freed hundreds of caskets, which floated away or became macabre parts of driftwood stuck nearby.

"What are you going to do?" asked Quincy resident Jack Hiland, talking with the *Chicago Tribune* as he prepared fresh catish for the skillet. "Are you going to stop living... working? You gotta keep on living; you gotta keep on working."

In August, Quincy, Mass., worked on helping its sister city, Quincy, Ill., keep on keeping on, sending more than 175,000 pounds of canned food, rice and juice as part of a "Mass Drive For The Midwest." That coalition of unions, businesses and the Salvation Army sent a caravan of 30 28-foot tractor-trailer rigs full of food and supplies to the Heartland.

The barge traffic that usually passes Niota and hundreds of river towns was shut down-- as were the trains, and many bottomland routes of area highways. But folks like Ford remain philosophical about their homes and why they live so close to such inconvenience and danger.

"The river is always scenic, and a lot of people come to our area-- all up and down the river-- to look at the river," Lynn says. "Some people want to see the Mighty Mississippi.

"And I emphasize mighty."

After standing for weeks in Niota's 90 houses, the Mighty Mississippi finally retreated enough to permit a 10-foot shredding machine to chop remains of the town's damaged contents into bales of refuse destined for distant landfills. Meanwhile, the local debate is whether to rebuild or relocate.

"You hear about the vanishing American farm," Niota antique store owner Carol Hogan told reporters. "On the river, it's going to be the vanishing American small town."

Ford argues that a once-in-a-lifetime disaster shouldn't discourage Niotans.

Pepsi-Cola General Bottlers, Inc.

1215 N.E. Adams Street
Peoria, IL 61603
(309) 676-4751

A heart attack
WAITS
FOR NO
ONE

In an emergency, every second counts.
No time for uncertainty. Immediate diagnosis
and treatment are critical. When you're
having a heart attack, time is not on your side.
At Proctor, we take chest pain and heart
attack symptoms seriously. *So should you.*

Call us for more information about
Proctor's Emergency Chest Pain Center
691-1070

PROCTOR
HOSPITAL

"The things we all have to keep in mind, though?" he said to town meetings. "This was a freak situation."

Months ago-- a day before the levee would break, letting some six feet of water rush almost 200 yards south to the bluffs overlooking Niota-- Ford doesn't yet appreciate the frightening freakishness. Instead, he's thankful.

"I truly believe that... Well, you know, a lot of people say that there aren't a lot of good people left in this country," Lynn says. "There's a lot left. Yeah."

Like a good dog
and a cold drink

(BRYANT)-- In southeast Fulton County, this town's gone to the dogs, one could say.

(I won't.)

Because Mary Bryan-- spelled without the T the town uses-- might be man's best friend in this village of about 400 people. In a couple of ways.

First, in a barn-red mobile home on the highway across from the railroad tracks north of town on Route 100, this petite entrepreneur grooms and boards... poodles.

"I've been in business since 1967, and I'd be safe in saying there are 400 or 500 in the county," Mary says, "house pets-- toy and miniature, usually.

"I also have people from Peoria, Mason County, up around Galesburg, all boarding dogs here in the summertime.

"People from all walks of life own poodles," she continues. "You have younger, older. It's just not the rich people who own poodles anymore. It's all classes of people. At one time, they used to be a rich man's dog, but no more."

Change begets change, Mary figured. So she diversified. She started a bar: Mary's Doghouse. Her tavern's name, oddly, is unrelated to poodles, she claims.

"The reason I came up with the name of Doghouse was because most guys who go out drinking are in the doghouse when they get home," she says, smiling. "But now I get people calling down there for appointments all the time. Then they refer them to the number up here."

After all, amid all of life's changes, some things are constant. Like a good dog and a cold drink.

Talking about boarding dogs or... bored Doghouse patrons, Mary concedes those at the bar occasionally... "need a leash." Or maybe overnight boarding.

"Well now, sometimes you think you're going to if you can't get them out," she says, laughing.

The wind wails through Mary's auburn hair. An empty shed and pen and run out back look a little... lonely.

"With all of the mines shut down and everything around here, it has a big toll on a lot of businesses," she says. "And business has fallen off quite a bit, with Caterpillar, because that's hurt a lot of people in this area, Caterpillar has. And then we had the mines close down; people have moved away. There's a big difference."

Then she sighs and smiles at the sublime-to-ridiculous turn her dog trade has taken.

"I used to breed; I don't (breed) any poodles anymore," she says. "I'm mainly raising Rotweillers now. They're becoming a popular breed right now."

Meanwhile-- such market forces notwithstanding-- traffic, maybe the world, seems to pass by... along with long, dark V's of geese flying over, leaving their winter grounds at the abandoned strip mines, heading for other places.

Memories made of this

(LACON)-- Driving north on Route 26 into Marshall County, motorists may find memories easing back into their minds. The relaxing wooded road and serene river views are calming there, almost hypnotic. It helps one remember.

And then-- between here and the Sun Foundation headquarters a ways south of town-- is... "Memories", a small spread of barns, sheds, chicken coops and other buildings inviting customers "to explore," according to Johnna Tallman.

"When you go out the back door, you go next door, there are 10 buildings, barns of different sorts," Johnna says. "We have furniture in the rough, we have tools, we have glassware, we have architectural items, used merchandise, just about anything you'd want has got to be over there."

Indeed, there are dozens-- hundreds-- of chairs and beds, coin-operated machines and knick knacks shelved and stacked and hanging from rafters. The large inventory is partly a result of the experience of Tallman and her partner, Joseph Cotten. They've been buying and selling merchandise and material from estates and auctions and individuals for years here and there, Johnna says.

"We've done shows for a long time, and they were very successful, but they were a lot of work-- plus a lot of money. For a good show, your rent can run $300-$400 for a weekend. So we decided we better put it in our own building. Since we had the access to the 10 buildings here, we felt that it would be a good place to put the (new) building. It's a little out of the way, but a beautiful drive, and if they ever get the roads done, it'll be very easy to get here."

Walking through the modern metal building used as a showcase for some of their showpiece antiques, cherry wood reproductions and brass fixtures, a visitor asks about the attraction to antiques.

"For antiques? It's just a love-- like an alcoholic, I guess," Johnna says. "I like the new merchandise, too, (but) I've been collecting for 25 years. I grew up with it, and it's just something that you dearly love."

Part of it, too, might be recapturing past time, special... memories.

"That's right; that's exactly right. Sentimentality," Johnna says. "I had someone here the other day and he saw something and said, 'My Lord! That's what my Grandmother used to have!' and he had to have it.

"And I said, 'You're hooked.' And that's just about what it is. You do say 'My Grandmother had one' or 'My Mom had that' or 'I remember growing up with that,' and you get kind of interested in it. And you start finding out more, and you start collecting."

The items and their popularity run the gamut, Tallman says, from elegant Victorian furniture to raucous art deco pieces; from exceptional silver to ordinary lighters.

"Everything goes in cycles," Johnna says. "Glassware was dead for awhile, and we've just sold a massive amount of good glassware."

Collectors also can be lured or driven by more obscure items, Johnna says.

"I have a man who buys nothing but old kitchenware, green-handled kitchenware," she says. "That's all he collects; he could tell you every piece. How he ever got started on it, I don't know.

"I had a lady in here the other day who collects old wrenches. That's all she collects. She says she's got probably 300."

And, once in a while, Johnna and Joe see a personal craving met, a dream fulfilled, almost.

"I had a caster set, where they had the vinegar and the different pieces," Johnna says, "I had just purchased it from an estate. A lady had been looking-- she had had her Grandmother's but it had gotten broken. The whole stand was glass. And I had just put it out and she was almost in tears, she was so thrilled, so elated.

"She had looked for 19 years, and she was just beside herself," she adds. "So, yeah, it's fun when they really find something. She was a very, very happy lady."

Memories revived.

Junk in the 'jungle'

(DAHINDA)-- As sturdy and stationary as the big red rock she moved here from a nearby hollow, Naomi Jones stands strong-- and tries to help others get on their feet.

"A long time ago, I just decided I wanted to do something different," Naomi says, shrugging off the cold as she stokes the small coal furnace in her home and business. "If people feel bad, I tell 'em, 'When you start out at the bottom, you can keep on going'."

Naomi herself has kept on going and shown others the way. From a cluttered, two-acre spread sprawled along Route 150 about a mile southwest of town, Jones heads up a clan-- a brood of children, grandchildren and guests. The daughter of an Apache woman who was brought to Illinois against her will, she says, Naomi takes care of her husband Charles, a disabled veteran, and various visitors in need.

Speaking about the time she gave up her room so that two neighbors could stay after their own home had burned, the 72-year-old Jones said, "It's kind of inconvenient-- being involved in other people's problems-- but what else can I do?"

What else? Usually, Jones barters and gets things-- and gets things done.

"I'm a born trader," she says, sighing deeply and smiling. "I hardly buy anything."

This two-story outpost used to be a gas station, grocery store and highway cafe serving the busy east-west traffic and its many tractor-trailer trucks, she recalls.

"After the Interstate (came through), we closed the restaurant and were going to call it 'The Trading Post,'" she says. "But, then, we decided to just be Jones' Bait Shop."

Dangling from a weathered cord by a window is a hand-lettered sign reading, "Pull rope for worms."

Besides bait, there's pop and ice, and there's antiques and collectibles and... junk. A few yards away sit farm implements from the horse-and-wagon era, a few tools and a couple of totem poles Naomi had carved from two utility poles she got.

"Oh, I like junk," she says. "I get it and I end up not wanting to move it. Just keep it. When I go, they'll probably have to pile it up on top of me.

"(The place) was a real jungle when we got it," she adds, pushing her glasses back up her nose. "We fixed it up;

added some rooms, a counter and some stools, two bath-rooms for the diner, and a bunch of bedrooms."

Now, Jones says she attracts about 1,000 people for each autumn's Spoon River Drive.

Dozens of hatchets hang from a wall next to the back-door entrance to her tidy kitchen and her living room, which is filled with a few "cigar-store Indians," plus busts and paintings, prints and postcards and photos of Native Americans.

"I'm part Indian," she says, "and my sons all give me these things. I raised five sons here. I'm still here."

Naomi hasn't strayed far from her childhood home, she says.

"I grew up across the road, where my parents lived for years," she says, bending and peering through a plastic storm window. "It was quite a childhood. I've never been out of the state, and I only went to school for about eight years. We started with nothing, so things got better.

"We'd carry water to the house, dig a little coal, gather wood," Naomi continues. "We'd run a mile or more back into the timber and pick berries and sell to people who drove by.

"That's when I learned to trade," she says. "My two sisters and three brothers and I would have a roadside stand with berries, plus squash and tomatoes and cur-rants, holding out a can for people's coins."

Even without much money, Naomi and her extended family have always done alright, she says.

"I just don't hardly fool with cash," she says. "First, there's not much money to mess with, and I love to trade. We get along fine."

They butcher their own meat from the livestock they raise in its own menagerie of sorts. There are pigs and pigeons, sheep and rabbits, goats and ducks, cats and a lone hunting dog, barking as he stands atop his doghouse.

"Mostly we live off the land-- the way things are sup-posed to be," Naomi says. "We raise chickens and grow vegetables. The kids pick up worms for bait."

Outside, there's a field filled with iron and wooden wheels, many milk cans, big saw blades, a wood pile, a hay rack, bikes in a rusted rack, tractor seats, and even five tractors. Nearby, a cannon fashioned from a stovepipe and a couple of scrap wheels points aimlessly over ornaments such as peeled-back tires with snow-covered flower beds, five cement deer, wooden tulips and miniature windmills and weather vanes, big kettles, hundreds of rocks and dozens of pumps.

"We're pretty proud of our pumps," Naomi says. "We have some ol' wind-ups and a railroad pump that serviced steam locomotives."

Walking up a driveway paved with bricks from the defunct Galesburg Brick Co., the trader indulges in a little philosophy.

"When you're buying, price is everything," Naomi says. "I go to a lot of auctions and come away with little boxes of goodies for 50 cents or so. You have to stick around and wait for the anxious buyers to leave. Bad weather's good. You have to have patience; most people don't.'

As an example, Jones points to a recent purchase: two tiny buildings, maybe originally toolsheds or pens, she bought for $2.50.

"Heck, I can use them for firewood at that price," she says, grinning. "We've always gone our own way. If I won the lottery tomorrow I wouldn't buy any new stuff. I'd go to a few sales and buy some junk."

Beyond the lot and behind a picnic table and three swing sets, a ewe bleats, fussing over a black sheep born in the barn that morning.

Photo by Linda Henson

Cliff Ganson and friend.

People ▬▬▬▬▬▬

Comedian Fred Allen is quoted as saying, "To a newspaperman, a human being is an item with the skin wrapped around it."

--Press Cuttings

I disagree.

Most journalists are unfairly stereotyped as unfeeling cynics by media cliches: the hard-drinking, desperate "ink-stained wretch" scrunched beneath a Trilby hat in a smoke-filled newsroom. Truthfully, reporters see people as readers and neighbors as well as subjects of stories. What CAN be sacrificed under the pressure of competition and deadlines is the "news value" of the common occurrence or the ordinary person who works and plays, raises kids and pays taxes, gives to charities and saves a piece of the American Dream through his or her life. Here are some worth noting.

Animal lover

(BARTONVILLE)-- Not far from the Greater Peoria Airport lives a white-haired man who's quietly devoted most of his 77 years to raising, showing, judging-- loving-- animals.

"I've had a couple pygmy goats and I've had deer-- all different kinds of animals and birds," says Cliff Ganson. "I've had 12 varieties of bantam chickens and six or eight varieties of pheasants, and pigeons of all kinds-- racing pigeons. We had one come home from 1,000 miles away, a homing pigeon. Then the next week he got killed by a coon."

Ganson was born in Manito, grew up in Pekin and Peoria, worked for decades at Prairie Farms dairy and married and had a family. Through it all, he says, were his animals.

"We were married 14 years before we had any children," Cliff says. "We were interested in running around to dog shows. My wife tells me I spend all my time out there-- that's where I belong.

"It takes time to take care of them and (in) bad weather, it's kinda hard," he concedes. "My age is keeping me down a little, (but) it's something to do. You never have an animal that talks back to you. I get along fine with them. They've all got personalities-- even the birds."

Frieda Ganson sits and smiles and urges Cliff to reflect on his beginnings.

"I guess I started out with them when I was about eight years old," Cliff says, "just puppies and small, fancy bantam chickens and things like that. Even in the Army, when I was in Hawaii, I had a dog over there that had puppies.

"I've had the dogs practically all my life," he continues. "I've handled all breeds for about 20 years before my legs went bad, then I started judging dogs. I don't have a lot of judging assignments-- I'm not that well known-- but I have a few, here and there, occasionally."

After some health problems, Frieda and Cliff cut down their animal activities to two boxers, which remind him a bit of their cherished Cookie, their first champion-- one of their very few companion animals, Ganson says.

"From time to time, we've had about five different ones altogether in the house, and they were all real close to us," he says. "I guess maybe that's one reason we don't have any in the house right now. The time each one of them passes away, why, it's a very heart-breaking experience to myself and my wife. So when the last one passed away we had in the house, that was another reason didn't want to. It was just like losing five children."

Despite such... well, tragedies, really, Ganson says he wouldn't do it differently, and he recommends parents help their kids learn about life and about caring for other people by caring for animals.

"I think that having animals or pets-- not necessarily dogs, but any kind-- is one of the greatest things that a child can do," Cliff says. "Because when children are small and wrestle around or fight, you teach them to behave and respect an animal the same as they would another human being. Live with them, learn to take care of them, have a little bit of responsibility to feed them and clean them-- it's a great thing for children. It teaches them while they're growing up that there are other people and animals on this Earth besides them-- to respect them."

Volunteer firefighter

(HAVANA)-- Small towns take pride in a peculiar sort of self-reliance, one that actually depends on the "kindness of strangers" (as Tennessee Williams wrote)-- or the kindness of neighbors.

For one of communities' basic self-services is the volunteer fire department, outfits which rely on folks willing to leave their jobs on a moment's notice to pitch in and help out in potentially dangerous situations.

"It makes you feel like you're doing something for the community, not just yourself," says Ron Campbell. "I mean, we're doing it to help our community out."

Campbell is a firefighter here, where three separate fires in the last year have severely damaged four buildings and nearly destroyed Havana's Main Street business district. More than 100 volunteers from more than a dozen area fire departments responded to help contain and extinguish each blaze-- the biggest in a decade.

Injuries were thankfully minor, mainly smoke-inhalation, but the fires were traumatic, Campbell says.

"It's upsetting that we lost so many buildings," Ron says. "There are times when you can fight it with as many companies as you can get, and you just can't stop it. It's sad. But we just try to do the best we can, the way we've been trained.

"We're glad we got it stopped where we did," he adds. "When we get it out and we stop any more damage from being done, that makes us real happy."

Campbell, a blond, 23-year-old Havana native, for more

than two years has been a volunteer and a firefighter with the local Fire & Rescue squad. There are 21 volunteers here, he says, plus a handful of full-timers on day and night shifts.

They keep busy.

"We have training every month-- the first Tuesday we have training, and the second Tuesday we have a business meeting," Ron says. "Lately, we've had a Firefighter 2 class that meets one day a week.

"The main thing is to teach other people that you've got to prevent these things," he adds, "(but) if they do happen, what to do in the event."

Wearing wire-rimmed glasses and a blue uniform with badges and patches, Campbell encourages people to participate in such a vital public service.

"Anybody that's interested can come in and get an application," Ron says. "If we've got room for them, we'll review their application. The trustees will do an interview and if the trustees approve them, they'll bring them up in front of the volunteers and we'll vote on them."

As the radio scanner behind him squawks, Campbell concedes there are... contradictions in his work.

"At the same time you don't want to have to do it, you WANT to do it because that's your job," Ron says. "It's interesting. It's odd to say-- kinda weird-- but it's fun. It's hard work at times, but we like doing it."

'Mister Twister'

(PEORIA)-- Forty-year-old Wayne Miller adjusts the volume on the radio between the bucket seats of his Plymouth Voyager. We're driving and watching the sky, which is slate gray but not threatening-- especially compared to a typical trouble call for Miller and about 100 other storm spotters in central Illinois.

"What do we do? We go out and look for tornadoes-- big

storms," Wayne says, laughing. "The National Weather Service is somewhat limited in that their radar pictures are a little bit old. So when they think they see something-- or the general public spots something-- we'll go out and look, and either confirm or deny that something has actually occurred, or if there's a particular storm cell in a given area."

Coordinating 16 central Illinois counties, the National Weather Service and the local Emergency Services and Disaster Agency rely on such volunteers. It can be exciting, Miller says.

"The last tornado that I saw was a couple of years ago up north of here, in a thunderstorm at night, and the only reason I saw it was because about six lightning bolts went off at the same time," Wayne says. "It was like that classic movie image of the funnel sweeping across Kansas. That's what they look like.

"I had one go right over the top of me once," he continues. "You get in the middle of one in a car like this, and you know it. It looks like the wind is coming at you from all directions. Then you hear the sound-- like a freight train, or 100 airplanes flying over at the same time."

This area might be "Tornado Alley," Miller says-- much of the Great Plains is. But there's a danger in treating twisters as commonplace-- taking them for granted. That "calm before the storm" cliche is real when dealing with the deadly force of a funnel storm, he says.

"I think all through the Midwest, this whole area can be called Tornado Alley," Wayne says. "We've been real fortunate in Peoria, because most of the stuff we've had over the last two or three years has gone either north or south of us. So we haven't had a lot of activity. But that's usually when people let their defenses down and don't think it's too serious, and that's when something sneaks in and really does some damage-- when you're not prepared for it."

Miller and his cohorts ARE prepared, he says. There's also a curious mix of the boredom of a stakeout and the adrenalin rush of a chase.

"We sort of have a contest amongst ourselves, to guess what time it's going to occur," he says. "We'll call each other on the radio and guess, based on how the day feels, on how the weather feels at the time."

"The Weather Service will give us some advance warning of a front; almost everything we get will come up through Missouri. So they can look and see if this is here and traveling at this speed, by this time this evening we're going to have some type of activity. So we just go out and wait for it, in a lot of cases."

Technically untrained, Miller's curiosity and enthusiasm helped him build some expertise, he says.

"This is all experience," Wayne says. "I like storms. I'm the guy who'd be out there with a camera taking pictures of a tornado while everybody else was hiding in the basement."

Miller's co-workers tease him, he says, but he just laughs-- and listens for the next alert.

"To this day, if there's a cloud in the sky when I walk into the office, they'll say, 'Well, is today the day for the Mother of All Storms?'" Wayne says. "It's fun-- plus I love storms.

"We have a lot more than people know about, but most are at night and don't touch the ground, so that's why there are no reports of damage. They're up there."

Blues voyage

(QUAD CITIES)-- Patrick Hazell cruises.

Whether playing on a Mississippi River steamboat or in some Midwest blues bar with the decor of a sailing vessel, the 47-year-old Iowa musician makes headway. He advances. Explores.

That's an achievement because Hazell seems to steer wide-- wild-- down the challenging channels of the music business. He's a road soloist who's also an occasional band member and studio musician. He resists technology but uses a lot of his own original hardware. And he's a self-taught player who values education-- as a workshop leader and teacher himself.

Music, he says, is his rudder. His anchor.

"Music itself is the bottom line," Patrick says. "It has to be enjoyable -- to hear and to play. It's not just about winning contests. That's why I'm always trying to add, to explore a different aspect of music."

A husky guy with fists like hams, Hazell's performances have him pounding at the piano, one leg bouncing against a bass drum beneath the keyboards. A cymbal shakes with the rhythm; a trumpet and tambourine lie within easy reach. Hunkering over a harmonica hanging on a holder, maybe blowing a few notes, Hazell leans back and un-leashes a gruff voice that wails about woes and wonders like work and love.

"I look at music differently than some musicians," Patrick says. "Music isn't much different than any of the arts: painting, writing, poetry. A musician can do creative, meaningful things, and those have nothing to do with playing in bars or not.

"I play all situations: bars, weddings, private parties, concerts," he adds. "Of course, I won't do some moody im-provisation in front of a cake party. It depends on the situation and what's happening."

That commitment also is how Hazell came to be con-ducting elementary and primary school workshops and holding a twice-weekly high school class in Washington, Iowa, he says.

"A teacher there asked me for ideas, and I told him that the traditional way of teaching music was bogus," says Hazell, who's in his sixth year there. "I'm totally untrained -- in every respect. Everything I've gotten is from doing it and from the people I've played with. So I have the students write songs and play in front of their peers. It's enjoyable."

Hazell-- the father of two sons and a daughter who are either in or done with college-- appreciates family, he says. And that extends from his own home to his loyal audiences and his former group, Mother Blues, which occasionally reunites for local appearances.

"There seems to be interest," he says about the Iowa City outfit that from 1968-83 also featured bassist Rick Cicalo,

47

drummer Steve Hayes, saxophonist Dan Magarrell and guitarists Joe Price and Bo Ramsey.

"I guess we achieved some kind of longevity."

Playing separately in Muscatine last Labor Day, Hazell and Price joined Ramsey onstage, and both the crowd and the performers liked the sound and the feeling.

"It went real well," Hazell says. "From the feedback I've gotten, I think it was the highlight of the day. And the chemistry was significant."

The chemistry has been a big part of Mother Blues' and Hazell's live shows. But they all rely on the music, which continues to evolve within the unchanging comfort of basic blues.

"It's hard to truly change, to be completely different," Hazell says. "There's always a sense of continuity. It's not like a watercolor painter suddenly using clay. It's more like a writer moving from longhand to a computer. An astute observer could see the same personality."

Computers-- or synthesizers, sequencers or any of a hundred technological devices-- aren't part of Hazell's music, he says.

"I'm a technological dinosaur," Patrick says. "People can't even buy anything I'm using. Onstage, I'm basically straightahead piano, bass drum, harmonica. However, I'm always recording something or another. So I'm not unappreciative of gadgetry. In fact, my major creative project for the year is a new studio."

Other projects on Hazell's horizon include more recordings, more trips to Germany (where he's already toured six times) and more miles logged on his '86 Chevrolet utility truck.

"It can seem crazy," he says. "But the music keeps things on an even keel."

Bocci ball champ

(WASHINGTON)-- On the north side of town, in the inviting den of a Bloomington banker's home-- on top of the color television set, beneath some Cubs memorabilia-- sit six special trophies. They're Alfred Biagini's. And they're for bocci ball.

"Well, I've been playing bocci ball on Sundays probably for 30 years," Alfred says. "During the summer, we have a regular league that plays every Sunday, from about April to October. And we travel around to a lot of small towns like Toluca and Standard and all those little old Italian towns where they used to play. But now it's gotten to be where there's more who're not necessarily of Italian heritage that are out there starting to play."

Biagini goes to Toluca-- along with hundreds of other players from towns such as McNabb and Mark, Ladd and Varna, Cedar Point and Winona.

"They used to play up there before, and Clitch Capponi, one of the old-time players, died," Alfred says. "So now they play and it's kind of in memory of him.

"It used to be, years ago, bocci ball was played next to a tavern on sand courts. Now, with the number of teams-- in Toluca last year we had 160 men's teams and close to 60 women's team-- they play literally all over."

Alfred, 61, adjusts his glasses and reflects on the attractions of the game.

"First of all, it's the fact that it's played in nice weather," Alfred says. "And it's the competition, trying to defeat the other guy, like in any other sport.

"Depending upon the ground-- especially in the spring when it's kind of soft-- people who can raise that ball high, it's kind of like golf, dropping the golf ball on a green, (do well). The higher you can raise it, it will roll very little. Some people can't raise it, and have to throw it stronger and keep it lower and have it roll quite a bit. So there's a lot to the game."

Just back from the state tournament in Springfield, Biagini smiles with pride and tries to stay humble about his bocci achievements.

"Me and my partner have finished first in Toluca-- or split-- twice, and we finished second in the state a couple of years ago," Alfred says. "Then we've won a lot of the small tournaments."

There are prizes and purses and, yes, trophies at tournaments-- and big crowds at events like Toluca's. It means a few hundred dollars to the winners. But it's not just the money. There are other thrills, Biagini says.

"I think it's putting it right next to it, and beating a team you know is darned good."

Firefly wrangler

(EDELSTEIN)-- Seated on a porch swing at his rural home, 12-year-old Ted Ehnle looks out over the garden and shed and barn, and recounts how he became a bug wrangler, rounding up fireflies.

"Ever since I can remember my family's been doing it," Ted says. "For about 10 years, I guess. My grandmother saw it somewhere in a magazine, I think."

The slim, brown-haired boy-- along with his five brothers and sisters-- sends containers filled with fireflies to St. Louis' Sigma Chemical Company, which coordinates a "Firefly Scientists Club" for church groups, 4-H Clubs, Scout troops and so on. In exchange for thousands of the insects, the company pays cash.

But Ted's not in this for the money, he says.

"They pay us a penny apiece for each firefly," he says, "(but) we just do it mostly for fun."

Ehnle-- who attends school in Dunlap-- has come to rely on a few... tricks of the trade, he says.

"We take nets to go out and catch them-- sometimes we use our hands and put them in the nets," he says. "We catch a whole bunch of them, then we bring them in. We put them in the refrigerator until they go into a semi-dormant sleep and don't move at all. Then you can count

Photo by Linda Henson

Alfred Biagini in action.

them and put them in the mailing containers that you send them in.

"We go a lot into the cornfields, because there's a lot of them out there-- until the corn gets too tall. Right when the sun goes down is the best time, because right after they light up, you can still see them. You only have about a half hour or 45 minutes; then after that, you can't catch them very good."

The chemical company uses two rare chemicals naturally produced in the tails of the fireflies, or lightning bugs, to study bacteria in waste water treatment facilities, plus medical research on heart disease, cancer and genetic disorders. So Ted has come to regard the bugs as... livestock.

He has affection for fireflies, and appreciates them, but he doesn't mind... sending them to market.

"It doesn't really bother me," Ted says. "I don't really feel bad about it. I just thought they were part of Nature. At least they can be used for something."

'People owe something to the public'

(CARTHAGE)-- Two tomato plants stand out back in a small, sunny yard behind the gray ranch house where Nancy Hendren quietly cultivates and coordinates her busy life.

She lives a few blocks east of the square here, but she seems to move in and out of the center of the community's many activities.

"I do a little gardening, but not much," she says from her patio. "I guess I have too many other things going."

Indeed, Hendren a couple of years back received the Lifetime Achievement Award from the area's Retired Senior Volunteer Program, which recognized her efforts to help others in a variety of ways.

"There was a little write-up in the local paper, and

Photo by Linda Henson

Ted Ehnle and firefly net.

people stopped me on the street and said, 'Goodness gracious! I didn't know you'd done all that!'

"But I just pointed out I didn't do it all at once. It took awhile. Years."

Hendren, 78, says she was young when she got a sense that people have an obligation to be involved.

"I got my start when I was about 10 years old, in 4-H," she says. "I really concentrated on 4-H for a few years, and through them I won a trip to Europe and met President Herbert Hoover.

"My father was a superintendent of schools in Menard and worked hard to send all us five kids to college. Along the way, he instilled in us that people owe something to the public, to use whatever talents they have to help others. Ever since I was a kid I've been involved with community activities or my church or my family-- whatever was most important at the time."

Nancy and her late husband, Paul, maintained two careers as they raised their children, something common today but rare decades ago. Paul was a teacher, then a veterinarian. Nancy worked with the Farm Security Administration, taught high school, then became a hospital dietician.

"I retired from Carthage Memorial Hospital in 1973, the year Paul died," she says. "But I never slowed down. I probably stepped up my activities."

Those activities run the gamut, from serious to frivolous, she says, but they all touch people.

Hendren has judged food fairs, taped readings for Western Illinois University's sight-impaired program, baked cookies for nursing homes and helped a catalog project at an area college. She's pitched in at the American Cancer Society and a local museum, the Presbyterian Church and the Republican Party and many other organizations and individuals.

Local folks describe Hendren as tireless and selfless, with a sense of humility and a sense of humor.

Bridge, reading and movies occupy the few spare moments Hendren schedules for herself, she says, conceding her schedule is demanding.

"Well, right now I'm lending a hand to the women's club PEO, which stands for Philanthropic, Educational Organization," she says. "And I know the Republican barbecue needs some organizing."

Hendren says she tries not to dominate opportunities to participate.

"I try to volunteer if no one else does," Nancy adds. "There was an elderly woman from church who needed a ride to Quincy, and I waited a couple of days to give other people a chance, too, because there are always people who want to help."

Hendren-- who gave the woman a ride when no one else stepped forward that time-- tries to play down the recognition.

"It's not false modesty, but I didn't want that award, except that it's the only one in west-central Illinois, so it kind of helps the organization," she says. "And I don't mind trying to be one, of a lot of local folks, who tries to set an example.

"You know, senior citizens should let their voices be heard, and do their share," she continues. "But it's also important to encourage young people to not just do what they like, but to help other people, too."

Bluebirds and happiness

(METAMORA)-- In a rural area west of town, a roadside mailbox featuring bluebirds greets a visitor. Opening the door, 52-year-old Marci Hoepfner is wearing a sweatshirt reading "Gem of Blue" and picturing a bluebird. Behind her is an entire wall devoted to bluebirds, with dozens of photographs and a few paintings. Shelves and counters are covered with books and magazines and newsletters from groups like the North American Bluebird Society.

Outside the Hoepfner kitchen window hangs a feeder labeled "Bluebird Cafe," where a few Carolina wrens are eating. Marci has business cards that say-- with no understatement-- "The Bluebird Lady of Metamora."

"We put specially designed bluebird nesting boxes up in the proper habitat, which is in the rural areas where there is scattered trees, more or less in open areas," Marci says. "They have to be 300 feet apart for the bluebirds' territory, in order to find enough food to feed their babies throughout the summer."

In scattered wilderness sites throughout Woodford County, Marci and her husband, Don, 54, have placed dozens of nesting boxes for the beautiful, subtle, endangered species. About the small, light-blue-and-orange birds-- which migrate to the Midwest for an April-to-August residency-- Marci has said, "they have the sky on their backs and the earth on their breasts."

She explains, "My husband designs the houses and then I take care of them throughout the summer. The houses are specially designed with 'attraction dots' to attract the bluebird when he comes in the area looking for nesting places."

Riding a tiny motorscooter she calls (what else?) the Bluebird Express, Hoepfner totes tools and camera gear, binoculars and books-- all to closely monitor her untamed but trusting... subjects.

"I keep detailed notes on my bluebird houses," Marci says. "Each of my houses is either lettered or numbered so that I know any day throughout the summer what's going on in each house. For instance, I can tell you when a nest was started, when the first egg was laid, when the babies hatched and also, when the babies reached 12 days old. (Then) I make a note of that so I know I cannot open that box again until after the babies have fledged at day 17.

"Then, it is very important to get in there and clean out that old nest, because Mrs. Bluebird will not reuse that old nest," she continues. "If you do not remove the nest, she will more than likely go in and start building a new nest on top of the old, which is not advisable because it raises the top of the nest right up even with the entrance hole. That makes it real handy for cats and coons to reach in and have a free dinner."

Photo by Linda Henson

Marci Hoepfner and feeder.

Instead, the protective Hoepfner has supervised generations of young birds-- almost 100 last summer alone. For her efforts, Marci has received recognition from birdwatchers, conservationists and environmentalists, and she's been awarded a national honor from the Izaak Walton League of America.

But what makes Marci warmest in the off-season are her own oil paintings, planning for her bluebirds' spring arrrival and Nature's many flying creatures.

"In the winter time, me and my husband enjoy watching many different varieties of birds-- chickadees, goldfinches, downy woodpeckers and the red-bellied woodpeckers," she says. "We're also blessed with a visiting male Tom Turkey occasionally."

Whether wild turkeys or Eastern bluebirds, all the winged wildlife here benefits from the hope and happiness in Marci's work.

Soft shoe, soft sell

(PEORIA)-- It's reassuring that in what's commonly thought of as a new and hectic, fast-changing world, a few old occupations still exist. In fact, they're still REQUIRED.

On Knoxville Avenue near McClure here, 68-year-old Luigi Vece is working on his sixth decade in the shoe-repair business.

"I've been in shoe repair since I'm eight years old," he says. "I've been in my own business here 12 years. I was down in Bergner's for 17 years, and I come from back East, in New Jersey, where I worked for somebody else. When I first went in the Army, I did it there for three months."

Luigi's training in the trade-- and its equipment-- came at the side of the masters, he says.

"I started with the old-timers from the old country-- from Italy-- not the fly-by-nighters," Luigi says. "You learn how to operate and everything else as you go along, 'cause there's somebody always there to teach you."

Within the soft roar of machinery that surrounds them, Vece and his wife work and wander around their shop, piled with shoes and suitcases, zippers of assorted sizes, and various odds and ends that people take for granted-- until they need fixed. Vece tinkers with a rumbling machine behind him, and he remarks that it'd be tough to start over in the 1990s, with today's new equipment.

"Well, it's more modern, but it's all basically on the same principle," Luigi says. "It's like cars. You get a 1919 car and compare it to a 1994, and they do the same thing. But they're different, see?

"The prices are outrageous (now, too)," he adds. "If you wanted to put new equipment in, you couldn't set it up for $50,000."

Since moving to Peoria from New Jersey in the '60s, Vece has coped with society's becoming more disposable, he says. But that hasn't hampered him or his trade.

"It's like anything else," Luigi says. "There's no such thing as less or more. It all depends on the capabilities and what you can do and perform. It's not only shoe repair. We do luggage repair, zipper repair, dye work.

"We can't quibble. We got more than our share of work, as you can see."

The Veces have benefited most from word-of-mouth recommendations, he says-- and loyal customers who keep coming back, appreciating not just Luigi's skills, but the trade itself.

"It's up to us to convince you to come here," he says. "We don't spend a dime for advertising, not a nickel since I've been in business."

Blues for the golden years

(PEORIA)-- Dark, carved wooden antiques stand in the corners outside the Mozart Room at the stately Jumer's Castle Lodge, where soft jazz Muzak is piped in through ceiling speakers, subdued lighting reflects off brass chandeliers and guests sink warmly into plush, stuffed cushions.

Toes tap a bit on the glazed brick floors of the foyer, and thoughts drift to subtle elegance. Into such surroundings strolls the oldest, darkest, most elegant piece of work around: Jimmy Binkley.

"Bill," he says in his distinctively raspy voice. He smiles. "Billbillbill."

His weathered, spotted hands reach out to shake, then smooth his hair-- combed straight back, then touch his neatly trimmed moustache and framed prescription sunglasses.

For more than 30 years, Binkley's hands have graced-- no, delicately danced-- across countless keyboards, entertaining thousands with an intimate, eclectic mix. He performs barrelhouse boogie woogie, sentimental standards and even timely novelties-- such as his original tribute to the city, "Forward Peoria".

"Ah," Jimmy sighs, like he's drawing a conclusion. "There's no better place to be."

Another season, another reason, recollect another scene: The morning sun shone through a spindly maple tree one spring outside the Lutheran Home, where a black man planned to play blues for graying white folks.

Binkley-- central Illinois' premier saloon musician-- wanted to celebrate his birthday by sharing his gift at three area nursing homes, and a couple of journalists tagged along.

"Where else would I be?" he asked, amused. "These people APPRECIATE it; I WANT to be here."

Binkley undoubtedly had celebrated his birthday at work-- he plays nightly at Jumer's Balkon Lounge-- but this was his first public acknowledgement.

"It's my BLANK birthday," he said then. "No age."

Indeed, this ageless artifact showed himself to be priceless.

He arrived carrying a plastic grocery bag of ice cream, and laughing like someone who knows too much.

"Ha, ha, ha... I love them," he said, greeting dozens of residents by circling the activity room, kissing cheeks and patting hands. "My little babies."

From hallways, some approached the room slowly, leaning on canes, walkers and each other. Nurses and aides wheeled others inside.

"A roomful of rockers," someone whispered.

Binkley sat down at the blond-wood Kimball upright piano and launched into a roadhouse stomp only vaguely recognizable as "Happy Birthday." Afterward, he surveyed the room and asked, "You remember this one?" and began "You're Nobody 'Til Somebody Loves You." Hands beneath comforters and quilts were coaxed out and clapped. Afterward, the applause became even more enthusiastic.

He unleashed "Blueberry Hill," "Pennies From Heaven" and "It Had To Be You," and he sang like he meant every syllable and note.

Someone brought over a cake with too-few candles and Binkley blew them out and readied to leave to play across the river at Fon Du Lac Nursing Home, then the Americana Health Care Center after that.

"Some of them just don't want me to go," he said, shaking his head as if he couldn't quite believe it. "I come here once in a while. Sometimes a gal will cry when I'm done. It's nice."

Jimmy will deny choking up himself. But during his

Photo by Linda Henson

Jimmy Binkley at the keys.

rendition of "As Time Goes By," dozens of pairs of eyes twinkled and he coughed a bit at the end and his sunglasses seemed to try to hide a tear swelling at the lid.

"It's paradise to be near you like this," he sang, his delivery too practiced and professional to quite crack, "because of you... "

And outside, there seemed to be buds on a couple of trees in the courtyard. And it seemed warmer than before.

Years and seasons later, a third scene was set.

It was summer lunchtime at Fulton Plaza, where hundreds of old people rode in vans and car-pooled and drove themselves downtown to enjoy one of Binkley's Senior Days, which add more color to people's Golden Years.

"This? They like my music, and they like getting out and doing something different," Jimmy said. "It all started when a lady was listening to me play at Jumer's and wanted me to come out to play at her mother's nursing home. I went out and played, and they enjoyed it and I enjoyed it. Now I go to one nursing home or another regularly."

Now, more than seven years later, Binkley on each of his Senior Days still hands out carnations from Millard's Florists in Edelstein, and gives away box lunches from Jumer's. They come from Lutheran Home and Fon Du Lac, of course, but also the Washington Christian Center and Peoria Senior World, St. Joseph's and Rosewood, Galena Park and Lindenwoods, Sharon Elms/Pines/Oaks and-- appropriately enough-- Good Samaritan.

One of Binkley's signature songs, one most of his many audiences remember, is "It's A Wonderful World."

And Jimmy helps make it seem so.

Horse trader

(KICKAPOO)-- Nine horses graze in a snow-covered pasture on a five-acre spread just south of town. Inside a comfortable brick home, Jim Lewis and his wife, Frances, welcome a visitor and talk about a vanishing breed: the horse trader.

"The horse trader that can say he's been in business-- and stays in business, not in today and out next week-- (is rare. The quitter) is not going to be a horse trader, and he's not going to get a reputation by going to a sale," Jim says, remembering his own youth, when he learned the business.

"We lived over by Galesburg, and we'd start there and come across country into Princeville, Dunlap, Laura and up around Victoria. We used to take horses behind a wagon-- that was the way we moved horses. We'd camp alongside the road, for a week. Everybody in the country would know, 'Well, the horse traders are around, we better go see what we can trade for.'

"You wouldn't move a lot of miles, and if you got a good spot, you'd stay awhile. Up here by Princeville, we stayed for 30 days one time, along the old lime quarry. We might have 40 horses on a day, and by the weekend, not have 15 of them."

The Lewises didn't just trade horses; they raised them, too. And also kids-- seven of their own and eight other youngsters they informally adopted.

"You know what kept them occupied? The end of a manure fork," Jim recalls. "You know-- 'You're going to ride that pony today, so don't pout about it. And don't say you don't want to ride him. You're going to ride him today and you're going to ride that horse, one one way and one the other way.'

"And they used to get pretty upset, but I said, 'That's your chore, so get it done, and then we're going to sit down and relax a little **while**'."

Lewis, 68, isn't exactly relaxing in retirement now. His hobbies-- fixing saddles and harnesses, going to rodeos-- revolve around horses. And his days are busy.

"I'm a lot better off out there, in the cold-- 'cause I dress warm, I take care of myself, eat good (and my animals eat good)-- than I am sitting in here watching the 'jukebox'," he says.

Photo by Linda Henson

Jim Lewis by his barn.

"I don't want to stay out of it. I've been in it so long that I'm known in Missouri, Indiana, Iowa and Wisconsin. In different localities, people know me and they, y'know, jingle the telephone.

"See, we go back past the turn of the century. My grandfather was in the horse business ahead of my Dad, and my Dad was in it 52 years before he passed away. I've been in it 51 years," he says. "I started out pretty young trading horses-- and it's still easier to lose $500 than it is to make $50."

Running his weathered hands through his white hair, Lewis recalls his own start as a horse trader.

His blue eyes dance.

"I sold one of my Dad's mules that was worth $150 or something, for $25, 'cause a guy come in and I knew that Dad had bought the mule for $20, and I thought, 'Well, if he makes five bucks, that's good'," Jim says, laughing.

"It's a high-priced schooling. You gotta have your thinking cap on all the time. I don't just buy and sell horses; I trade horses. I'd just as soon trade with you on a horse you got out here. If I got a horse you like, well, I'll take your old horse that you want to get rid of, in on trade. I got a place for him down the road."

There have been many roads, many miles since Lewis began to swap horses. His family sold most of the horses in Peoria 50 years ago, from milk wagons and the city stable to the Shelton gang. Riders and horse people remember him.

And that comforts him, Lewis says.

"The thing that makes me feel good is that I've got customers coming back here-- customers of my dear ol' Dad's when he was in business-- coming back with their great-grandkids and so on," Jim says. "I guess that's, y'know, the thing that I live by. I can still go out here and face people. I don't have to run and have a bodyguard with me or nothing else. And that's worth a lot."

Bogguss: rising star

(KEWANEE)-- Her eyes shown like liquid light, spar-kling and sparking with arcs of charged electricity.

"I hope nobody asks me to sing that danged hog song," said Suzy Bogguss, appearing here a few years ago. "It IS the Kewanee Hog Festival. But..."

Onstage in Kewanee or Knoxville or Nashville, Bogguss energizes audiences with her innocent ambition and her worldly but hometown charm. After all, several communi-ties claim the 36-year-old country music performer. Born and raised in Aledo, Bogguss also lived and worked and played in Galva, Galesburg, Bloomington-Normal, Peoria and here-- before committing to country music and mov-ing to Nashville.

In hindsight, long-time observers feel that Bogguss also exhibited a zeal and a zest for life she's showed at various venues: Dolly Parton's musical theme park and Peoria's Glen Oak Park, in Mexico City for a month-long gig or playing a night at a Bloomington bar for $7 plus all the pizza and beer she could consume.

"Suzy had something special, a spark, that no one else had," said music teacher Maurice Stephens. "She had musical abilities, but what really stood out was her personality: effervescent. And she was a complete social butterfly, a nonstop talker. She just sparkled."

Stephens-- himself a Peoria Woodruff graduate who learned music from the likes of Lawrence Fogelberg-- has taught hundreds of grade and high school students in Carthage and Aledo, International Falls, Minn., Janesville, Wisc., and now Sterling, Colo. Some of his former pupils became professional musicians, such as Bogguss-- who's won the Academy of Country Music's best new female vocalist (1988) and the Country Music Association's award for best up-and-coming artist (1992).

Other Stephens students also became accomplished musicians, such as Colleen Metternich-- Miss Illinois 1973. Still others became, well, journalists.

"You know Mister Stephens from Carthage?" Suzy asks,

her reserved smile revealing a hint of an overbite and a healthy dimple. "He liked 'rowdies' like you and me, didn't he? He cultivated talents. Any skills I have, he knew."

Stephens, who's seen Bogguss perform since her 1985 move to Nashville, says she was "a cut-up, always kibbitzing with my wife at rehearsals.

"But she was punctual and on pitch," he adds. "And she and her mother constantly volunteered to help with costumes and backstage details."

Bogguss says that her mother, Barbara Bogguss, was an inspiration.

"I'm a bit of a ham," Suzy says. "The stage is a comfortable place for me to be-- although I don't know if I could play Hamlet. Mom was a performer at heart. She was a drama major in college and quit to get married and have a family."

Growing up in west-central Illinois, Bogguss says her mom and dad (Bud Bogguss) exposed her to all kinds of music, from Big Band and country to pop tunes from the 1960s. Now, her favorite performers range from Linda Ronstadt and Emmylou Harris to Ella Fitzgerald and Paul Simon.

A pretty typical young American who sang in choir and went to Girl Scouts, Suzy says she learned about country music and westerns from playing her folks' Eddy Arnold and Patsy Cline records and watching "Fury" on television. The country connection suprised Stephens, he says.

"Suzy doing country music threw me," he says, laughing. "Folk music was understandable, but country? Yodeling? But she's carried it off; I actually think it's great now."

Capitol Records signed Bogguss to a development deal in 1986, and the next year released her first major-label record, a single of "I Don't Want To Set The World On Fire." A follow-up single, "Love Will Never Slip Away," paved the way for the release of her debut LP, 1989's "Somewhere Between."

Praised by listeners and reviewers (one described her sound as "cowgirl folk-pop with contemporary themes"), the record's songs were by Patsy Montana, Hank Williams, Merle Haggard-- and Suzy Bogguss.

Since then, Bogguss has released 1991's "Aces," which had three hit songs, and last year's "Voices In The Wind." Her output has varied from videos ("Drive South" and "Outbound Plane") to hit singles (a remake of Judy Collins'"Someday Soon" and "Letting Go"-- co-written with songwriter husband Doug Crider).

Lately, she's even branched out into non-musical endeavors, most notably the Suzy Bogguss Leather Collection, which came out on the West Coast early this year.

Bogguss takes any achievements in stride, she says.

"I'll enjoy whatever successes come along," Suzy says. "It's a series of steps; it's better than moving too fast. I don't want to find myself in deep water, back-pedaling in reverse to safety."

Getting in over her head has been unlikely for Bogguss for years. Before all of her albums and honors, before becoming a regular guests on cable's Nashville Network-- from "Nashville Now" to "Crook and Chase"-- and even before spending several years performing throughout Central Illinois, it was obvious to some insiders that Bogguss had the ability to take difficult or unusual material and successfully present it in an entertaining way that seemed all Suzy.

"She was involved in district and state music contests, but mostly I remember her playing Bonnie in Anything Goes,'" Stephens says. "She did a fantastic job in this very comic character. She always wanted to go a step further."

Bugguss returns the admiration.

"I got so much from Mr. Stephens," she says. "Sometimes I think of him when I sing because he'd always make us enunciate. After all, singing a melody is one thing, but people need to understand what in the heck you're saying. That's for danged sure."

The Past ━━━━━━━━━━

Washington Post editor Ben Bradlee said, "News is the first rough draft of history."

--Press Cuttings

If so, some "historians on the run" witness important events and try to put them in context, only to watch significance swept away by the avalanche of excitement. It's hard to tell if being a journalist is filled more with such frustration or with fortune. Newsman/writer Ben Hecht said, "Along with the endless saga of misfortune that hits the eye of the reporter, he gets to see the queer stamina of little people in big troubles. He is given a privileged look at the undaunted moments that are the soul of human history." The histories of two Illinoisans are summarized here, along with the National Pastime's lost roots-- in the Midwest.

Vagabondage:
Vachel Lindsay in disfavor

(SPRINGFIELD)-- Sixty-two years ago, Illinois writer/illustrator Vachel Lindsay committed suicide, leaving a legacy of literature and lore that starts in central Illinois, but extends across the globe.

A leading voice-- literally-- in the New Poetry of the early 20th century, Lindsay's birthplace, his deathplace, is a modest, two-story house on South Fifth Street in Springfield. Across Edwards Street from the Governor's Mansion-- a lush, landscaped estate of esteem and power-- the Lindsay structure stands weak, latched and locked, shuttered like it holds some shameful secret.

It seems hollow, if not empty.

"Well, it's been open the last two weekends," says Charlotte Oglesby, one of several temporary guides who led visitors through the house during the holidays last year. "Hopefully, we'll be open again in the summer."

Designed and built in 1840 by Henry Dresser-- who also built Abraham Lincoln's home here-- the house was purchased by the Lindsay family in 1878. It has 11 rooms and a bath and a half, all generally decorated in a dark, brooding style. Immediately inside the front door are steep steps leading to the second floor, with a carved bannister. The furniture is mostly original family items, including pieces made by a 13-year-old Vachel.

Opposite the rather repressive master bedroom is the long dining room/parlor/library, with a musty air of... privilege and intelligence, where many books and periodicals are stacked, copies of Lindsay's artwork are hanged, a large mirror is reflecting guests back at themselves and a top hat is placed on a night stand. The walls are covered with a textured material called raised fresco that's not fabric but seems so.

Upstairs, plaster is cracked here and there, but there's Lindsay's small room-- an austere corner overlooking the Governor's grounds, where William Jennings Bryan spoke during the presidential campaign of 1896, when Lindsay was 16 and watched, enthralled. There, in his room, an unpretentious writing desk is at the window, next to a traveler's trunk reading "Vachel Lindsay. Davenport Hotel. Spokane, Washington."

The room-- the home-- was a creative cauldron for Lindsay. Here was his birth and his youth, his visits and return in 1929, and the growth of his own family and his death. It's at once forbidding and forgiving, as visitors reluctantly cross the threshold into shadows, then slowly notice streams of sunlight and brightness illuminating areas where Lindsay wrote and drew and dreamed. Now, outside, the house's roof has scraped, scruffy asphalt shingles, the clapboard siding has peeling gray paint and the porch floor has tongue-and-groove planks as chipped and warped as Lindsay's reputation. The window shutters have broken slats; they've also seen better days. Inside, wood-plank floors and intricate woodwork hint at those better days-- days before Lindsay's rejection or ostracism, before the State's budget cuts forced its closing.

"It's not lack of interest," Charlotte says. "We had quite

Vachel Lindsay. (Photo courtesy of the Vachel Lindsay Association.)

a few people visiting very interested in the house. They come for various reasons: for Vachel Lindsay, because it's an old house, and others are interested in the architecture of the house.

"Improvements are being made," she continues, "and an in-depth study is being done to see exactly what has to be done as far as repairing the house."

The sidewalk shows cracks and the grass is flat from recent rains' runoff. Leaves lie strewn across the slight incline to the porch, where four four-by-four posts form a stable, if not stately, frontage. Nine windows face the street, on the east. It's a contrast conflicting with the manicured elegance of the Governor's Mansion, with gardens' greenery visible around the tall brick wall now separating its south side from the Lindsay residence.

Despite standing in the shadows of the Governor's Mansion, the house might be forgotten in the bureaucratic shuffle of priorities in the Illinois Historic Preservation Agency or state government itself, Oglesby concedes. But she's surprised Lindsay's poems were dropped from the Norton Anthology of American Literature, a basic English text.

"Many of us have studied his poetry-- especially his poems-- when we were going to school, in our English classes," she recalls. "That's the way I remember. I don't know if they do this today, but I know that in my time, you did study poetry, and he was one of the poets that you did study."

One of the so-called "prairie poets", along with Carl Sandburg and Edgar Lee Masters, Lindsay-- who "tramped" on foot across much of the continent-- generally was considered an... eccentric by Springfield during his life. After his death, his stature rose and fell with popular and critical attitudes and opinions. Although somewhat overlooked elsewhere, Lindsay still retains some local following, Charlotte says.

"Oh, I'm quite certain that those that like his work are proud," she says. "I mean, he had a different style. He was very unique. I think the more you read-- if you pay attention to what you read, as far as poetry's concerned-- eventually you'll get the style that he had. He was always trying to get a message across to the people.

"Those who know of him are impressed with his work," she continues. "Others are very interested when they come in. They see his art, which accompanies his poetry. And they realize that this was a very important part of... of--"

Oglesby's voice fades and she shrugs, perhaps in resignation, perhaps in rage at people's short memories, perhaps in irony. One of Lindsay's more memorable works was about Illinois Gov. John Peter Altgeld: "The Eagle Forgotten":

"Sleep softly ... eagle forgotten ... under the stone,

"Time has its way with you there and the clay has its own.

"Sleep on, O brave-hearted, O wise man, that kindled the flame

"To live in mankind is far more than to live in a name,

"To live in mankind far, far more ... than to live in a name."

Today, south of the city is the artificial Lake Springfield, near Spaulding Dam, spanned by a bridge dedicated on July 12, 1935: the Vachel Lindsay Bridge. But the home is a shut-down shrine, with dingy fabrics made less dreary only by dust motes. On my special visit to the house, I was at first cautioned not to touch anything. But after awhile, a guide led me to an off-limits area upstairs off the servants' quarters, where there's a tiny storage room.

I peeked in.

Inside this trunk room was the more mundane part of Lindsay's life, which went unnoticed by the local and the literary elites. Inside its cramped closet are many scrawls and scribbles: pencil notes recording gardening or sewing, shopping tips or when some wallpaper was installed, marks making make-shift measuring charts for children's heights, dates to remember.

Or forget.

Leaving, visitors notice brittle bridal-wreath bushes and other scrub brush dotting the lot, disregarded.

Baseball's roots reach to 1800s Illinois

Baseball's Hot Stove circuit was stoked, steaming with winter meeting conjecture, speculation about the expansion draft, dread about the threatened spring-training lockout and just plain awed that a team from outside the United States won the 1992 World Series.

It was a confusing time.

Maybe it's always been like this.

"You go through 'The Sporting News' of the last 100 years, and you will find two things are always true," said Don Fehr, director of the Players Association. "You never have enough pitchers, and nobody ever made money."

On the other hand, maybe the National Pastime is different.

After all, the World Series went a step toward becoming a true "world" series in 1992, as the Toronto Blue Jays became champions-- the first team from another country to do so. Despite superstations beaming games overseas via satellite, the Olympics' addition of international baseball competition and decades of major league clubs playing exhibition games against local teams in Japan and Central America, that global sense was unusual.

Meanwhile, the big leagues' newest clubs-- the Colorado Rockies and the Florida Marlins-- each picked 36 players for franchises that cost $95 million. That seems like a sum big enough to buy all of Europe's surplus seed oil, ship it through Bosnia and feed Somalia.

And not to be outdone in the sporting news-making front, baseball executives privately talked trades and owners openly practiced their collusion techniques for future season. That seems different. Bold. Dumb.

But in central Illinois, what's the same is the kid's game and the mature sport that developed more than 100 years ago, not only with teams such as Cincinnati's Red Stockings and cities such as Boston and Chicago, but with franchises in Rockford and Peoria. Much of baseball's history is humble, a heritage hailing from modest Midwest ballyards in the 19th century. There's a danger in forgetting that. Swept up in swift challenges to baseball, fans can lose the love of local lore. Reaching out might be great; growth fine. But in the excitement of expansion and novelty and doom, baseball needs to cherish its past.

Along the Illinois River, organized baseball was first recorded during the Civil War, when Peoria regularly fielded teams for contests played before hundreds of spectators. Shortly thereafter, ballplayers began to play for pay, usually from sponsors who arranged phony jobs for players to get money, or by dividing the gate receipts.

The professional Peoria Reds in the 1860s and '70s were led by Charles G. Radbourn, a young pitcher who also played for a semi-pro team in Bloomington. Eventually, Radbourn's 12-year career took him to Boston, Providence and other Eastern cities, where he earned the nickname "Old Hoss". But after baseball he returned to central Illinois, dying in Bloomington at the age of 42. He was elected to Baseball's Hall of Fame in 1939.

"The National Pastime" magazine called this picture "a remarkable find." Shown is Bloomington's semi-pro baseball team, circa 1875, featuring ex-Peoria Red and future Hall of Famer Charlie Radbourn (holding the ball in the middle row). (Photo courtesy of the Society for American Baseball Research: SABR.)

A fellow Hall of Famer who played Peoria in the 19th century was Joe "Iron Man" McGinty, who pitched for the Peoria Distillers in 1898 before eventually setting the major-league record for innings pitched in a single season (434) and double-headers pitched in one day (five).

Other Peoria Reds included St. Louis brothers Jack and Bill Gleason, who later starred for their hometown teams, and Jack Rowe, a slugging infielder who started out with an amateur team in Jacksonville and went on to the Rockford Forest City squad, then 12 more major-league seasons in Pittsburgh, Detroit and elsewhere.

There were many semi-pro outfits featuring community

teams from towns such as Chillicothe, Quincy and Galesburg (where Carl Sandburg played). Players in the Midwest and the East all struggled to financially survive in the game-- dubbed a "gentleman's sport"-- until it was officially raised to professional status in 1871 with the National Association (of Professional Baseball Players).

Then, there were nationally known franchises located in New York and Philadelphia, but also teams in Ft. Wayne, Ind., (the Kekiongas) and Keokuk, Iowa (the Westerns). In that Mississippi River town, the frustration of failure played itself out.

Literally.

"Keokuk (in 1875) won one out of 13 starts and quit," writes historian David Voigt. "Four other clubs, with the combined record of 17 wins and 88 losses, also chose to drop out."

That seemed to demonstrate players' profound disappointment, but it also just reflected an extremely unstable time for professional sports. Baseball's shaky league-- with as many as 13 teams from as far west as St. Louis-- experienced the effects of gambling as much as the wonders of talent. But its talent was plentiful. One of its exceptional stars was on the Forest Citys of Rockford: Albert Goodwill Spalding.

Born in Byron, Ill., Spalding started out pitching for local amateurs, then advanced to the semi-pro Rockford Forest Citys. That team first earned a place in baseball lore when they upset the powerhouse Washington Nationals during an 1867 tour "West" (as far as Illinois). That year, the East Coast club met the upstart Forest Citys at Chicago's Dexter Park, where the 17-year-old Spalding led his team to a Cinderella victory over Washington, 29-23.

"I knew that every player on the Rockford nine had an idea that their kid pitcher would surely become rattled and go to pieces as soon as the strong batters of the Nationals had opportunity to fall upon his delivery," Spalding recalled. "They had good grounds for that fear."

But to underscore Spalding's and the Rockford team's feat, the Nationals the next day drubbed the usually dominating Chicago Excelsiors, 49-4.

By 1871, Spalding's teammates on the Rockford club included Adrian "Cap" Anson (a future Chicago White Stocking star), Robert "the Magnet" Addy (presumed to have been the inventor of the slide) and Chick Fulmer (credited with baseball's first unassisted triple play). The only professional league, the National Association was the "major league."

But that initial season in that first pro league mainly meant that Rockford went down in the record books as the first last-place team in American professional sports, with a record of 6-21.

So fans may still wonder: How did a U.S. Marine color guard mistakenly parade with an upside-down Canadian flag? Why do owners whine about paying their players less than Garth Brooks or Madonna or Steven Seagall earn in their fields of entertainment? And who are Rockies and Marlins like Eric Wedge and Jesus Tavarez?

But we remember: it's the effort, not the results. And maybe the best thing about the past is, it's over.

E.W. Scripps: the heart of a dirt farmer

(RUSHVILLE)-- One of America's most colorful and controversial newspaper publishers and supporters of working people came from this Schuyler County community of about 2,000 people, who recall him and his family with fondness.

The family was Scripps.

The man was E.W. Scripps.

"People here look on the Scripps family with pride," says Alan Icenogle, editor and general manager of the Rushville Times daily newspaper. "They got their start here. Plus, the Scrippses still think of Rushville as their home. They come back, they mingle, they remember."

Last summer, Charles Scripps gathered about 250 relatives in a reunion marking the 200th anniversary of the family's arrival in the United States.

E.W. Scripps (1854-1926) probably would have appreciated the folksy charm of hundreds of residents milling with wealthy and influential members of the Scripps family. It's a relationship he cultivated and enjoyed during his decades of work as a newspaperman.

Scripps and the Scripps family started dozens of newspapers, the United Press wire service, Scripps-Howard News Service, and other media endeavors. The heads of the clan, William and Grace Locke Scripps, landed from England in July 1791.

Fifty-three years later, London Daily Sun publisher William Arminger Scripps followed his father and two brothers, George Henry and John, who lived in "an Illinois frontier town, Rushville," writes Vance H. Trimble in his biography, "The Astonishing Mr. Scripps" (Iowa State University Press, 547 pp.).

"The Londoner was captivated by the raw grandeur of the prairie and impulsively bought 160 acres one mile south of the Rushville courthouse," Trimble continues. "Edward Wyllis (Willis) Scripps was born June 18, 1854, with the heart of a dirt farmer, the soul of a poet, and the flaming brain of a crusading newspaper publisher."

In this, the first complete and candid Scripps biography, Trimble ties together not only the Illinois farm boy and the worldly philosopher/businessman, but also the philandering young man and lonely old tycoon, the fiscal conservative and the embittered blue-collar champion, the upright family man and the irresponsible alcoholic. Trimble lays the groundwork for Scripps' contradictions in Rushville.

E.W. Scripps' father, James Mogg Scripps, was a celebrated London bookbinder relegated to homesteading the humble spread outside Rushville. After all of the required work, he and his family retreated to books and discussed the issues of the day.

In 1858, four-year-old Eddie accompanied his father to town to hear Abraham Lincoln speak on the courthouse steps. Even in boyhood, "Eddie first became aware of the importance of newspapers," Trimble writes. "At the family hearth he had heard much of William Arminger Scripps' prominence as a publisher in London."

And branches of the family continued to grow in news-papers. Cousin John Locke Scripps helped set up the Chicago Tribune; another cousin, Benjamin Franklin Scripps, established the Prairie Telegraph; still another cousin, George Washington Scripps, launched the Schuyler County Citizen. The latter two newspapers merged and continue today as the Rushville Times.

E.W. was 18 when he boarded the CB&Q train car at 4:17 a.m. on Saturday, Nov. 2, 1872, to join his older brother James at his Detroit newspaper, the Evening News. E.W. started as a $3-a-week office boy, but worked his way through the circulation department to the newsroom, where James finally made him a cub reporter.

"The idea that my brother submitted to me was the publication of a daily newspaper, very small in size, with large type, and which, by reasons of having condensed writing, would contain all the news... found in the large blanket sheets' and sell it for two cents or a penny," E.W. later wrote.

Although the Detroit experiment was James' idea, it was E.W. who became the outstanding practitioner of setting up newspapers that were sensationalistic and cheap, yet aspired to stand up for the common citizen. E.W. achieved this skill from instinct and study. While still in Detroit, Scripps learning the internal and external workings of a circulation department, the challenges and woes of a jour-nalist and a manager, and the ideals and vision of an editor and publisher. He took his talents to Cleveland, St. Louis and Cincinnati, then Denver, Chicago and Baltimore.

He had formidible rivals.

In St. Louis, Joseph Pulitzer also embraced sensation-alism and crusading reporting in the *Post Dispatch*-- also espousing the cause of the working person. Pulitzer in 1878 had proclaimed his reform newspaper "will serve no party but the people... will oppose all frauds and shams, whatever and wherever they are; will advocate principles and ideas rather than prejudices and partisanship."

By World War I, Scripps had almost 30 papers, coast to

coast, including the *New York World-Telegram*. By the 1920s, Scripps' newspaper holdings were second only to William Randolph Hearst's empire.

"Hearst seems to be following me up pretty regularly, although he spends millions where I spend thousands," Trimble quotes Scripps from 1922-- when Hearst bought the *Baltimore American and News* to compete with Scripps' Post there.

"I was never quite bold enough to prophecy the failure of William R. Hearst," Scripps continued. "The farthest I ever went was to say that according to all my own principles and ideas, Hearst ought to be a failure. Instead, he has been more successful than I have been."

But in spite of fierce competition from other newspaper giants, Scripps prospered, his influence outpacing his fame-- which he sought to avoid.

"Locally, people think of E.W. as just one of the clan," remarks Icenogle of the Rushville Times. "But a lot of people also recognize him as the one who did the most, became the most famous, and made the greatest contributions to society."

One of the world's earliest newspaper chain owners, Scripps called himself both a "people's champion" and a "damned old crank." He instructed his newspapers' editors and managers to work to improve the status quo.

"Whatever is, is wrong," he said. "The first of my principles is that I have constituted myself the advocate of that large majority of people who are not so rich in worldly goods and native intelligence as to make them equal... in the struggle with individuals of the wealthier and more intellectual class."

To represent workers, E.W. attacked corruption in government and industry, greed by the trusts and monopolistic utility companies, and religious authoritarians. Like Horace Greeley, Scripps believed newspaper employees should own part of the company. So although he paid only average wages, he gave his editors and senior staff as much as 49 percent of each newspaper.

"I am one of the few newspaper men who happen to know that this country is populated by 95 percent of

plain... and poor... people and that (their) patronage is worth more to a newspaper owner than the patronage of the wealthy 5 percent," he said. "So I have always run my business along the line of least resistance and for the greatest profit, and... I have made money easier than any newspaper publisher did make it..."

Such candor is helped by Trimble's resources and style, which permit his subject to speak. Trimble, a 1960 Pulitizer Prize-winning reporter, had access to volumes of family correspondence and corporate communications. And he compiles and conveys the material in a conversational tone, making it readable as well as informative. Trimble is a long-time newspaperman whose books include the 1990 biography *Sam Walton: The Inside Story of America's Richest Man*.

A rich man himself, E.W. Scripps nevertheless crusaded against many establishment policies and against the economic system that supported the robber barons such as John Rockefeller, Jay Gould and Andrew Carnegie against the interests of the rest of the country. He also crusaded for the establishment of labor unions and collective bargaining. In fact, the chain's prestigious Cleveland daily, the liberal, pro-labor Press, in 1936 became one of the first employers to sign a contract with the upstart American Newspaper Guild, representing reporters. The result was the enmity of fellow newspaper publishers and appreciation (and new subscriptions) from the working class.

Although some of Scripps' papers have been sold or folded-- the *Baltimore Post*, papers in Buffalo and Houston, even the flagship *Cleveland Press*-- he persevered during his life as a gadfly. And some of his remarks are eerily timely.

"The wealthy people of the United States are damned thieves," Scripps wrote. "The rascality of the rich man has been used to influence Congress to rig the tax law with purposeful defectiveness to provide loopholes for the wealthy. My own millionaire class could more easily pay a 25 percent income tax than the 99 million common working men could pay 2 to 4 percent."

E.W. Scripps at his California compound. (Photo courtesy of Scripps-Howard.)

Today, this Western Illinois community has a working class, of course, but few labor unions, Icenogle says.

"We have quite a few building tradesmen and some city employees just organized to be represented by the Operating Engineers, but there aren't a lot of unions located in town," he said

E.W. probably would be disappointed-- as he would have about the 1992 strike that shut down his chain's *Pittsburgh Press,* leading to its loss through a merger with another daily.

"Whenever there has been a contest between the ruling classes on one side and the wage-earners on the other, I have chosen to be the friend, associate and fellow-striver of the second party," Scripps wrote. Speaking of his years growing up on a Rushville farm, he commented, "I always liked to work in the dirt."

The Present ━━━━━━━━━━━━

American journalist and humorist Finley Peter Dunne is credited with first stating in 1902 the ideal mission of the American press: "The job of the newspaper is to comfort the afflicted and afflict the comfortable."

--Press Cuttings

The news media's job performance is below average.

There's a phrase that the press has used so often in recent years that it's lost its impact: "Broken Heartland." As these pieces show, something's in need of repair, and it's more than roads and bridges. There's hunger in the land. However, there's hope as well. And whether it's welfare's heartbreak and sorrow or sharing's heartache and joy, people's needs and neighbors' responses are meaningful and important.

Habitat For Humanity: homes for humans

(PEORIA)-- Wearing a madris shirt and summer slacks, retired Caterpillar manager Ray Hettiger has escaped from a midday downpour, seeking shelter inside the modest headquarters of the Greater Peoria Area Habitat for Humanity at 813 NE Madison.

A longtime volunteer who recently coordinated a group of retirees in remodeling and rehabbing the offices in the old house here, Hettiger now is busy juggling other projects, demands, resources and people.

"Any volunteer organization greatly fluctuates according to the need," Ray says. "I would say we have a stable group of about 30 to 50 people. But we had 200 different people work on a recent house, so it fluctuates greatly."

With thin hair and a nice smile below his frame glasses, Hettiger gestures around the room to stacks of the non-profit group's newsletters, to piles of letters and memos and notes, and to some photos of other structures, other successes-- like some of the seven houses built or renovated throughout Central Illinois since Habitat formed in the late '80s.

"Three of our houses have been donated to us, that we've rehabbed," Ray says. "We have a committee-- I head up that committee-- that goes out and examines a house, and we do a cost estimate on it. And then we decide whether or not we can handle it. If we can, why, then, we go ahead and we do it.

"We have another man who's my counterpart who works on new house construction-- Don Baker, a carpenter," Ray continues. "We have a regular board; it's set up like any business, with various committees and that sort of thing."

Habitat's literature has slogans such as "Co-workers, not caseworkers" and "Capital, not charity." An international ecumenical effort, Habitat for Humanity has brochures that cite the Bible: "Our love should not be just words, and talk," John says. "It must be true love which shows itself in action."

"We have 25-plus churches supporting us here in the greater Peoria area," Ray says. "It's interdenominational-- Catholic, Baptist, Lutheran, etc.-- and I think that's one of the great things about Habitat, actually, is bringing all of these people together and we work in a common cause. And nobody really knows what the other person's religion is, it's just that we all work together to get the job done.

"We do have people who have no church affiliation at all that are some of our very best volunteers," he adds. "I can think of one fellow in particular. He's a hard worker, he puts in a lot of time with us on houses, he donates generously, but he has no affiliation. He just thinks it's something that has to be done."

Thousands of people have agreed since Millard and Linda Fuller in 1977 founded the Americus, Georgia-based Habitat for Humanity International. Assisted by the likes of Rosalynn and Jimmy Carter, Habitat's unique shared-work program requires homeowners to contribute an average of 250 hours of "sweat equity" in their new home-- and to help other prospective homeowners build their own homes.

Houses are built or renovated using as much volunteer labor and donated material as possible, organizers say. The dwellings are sold at no profit and no interest. Loan payments are recycled to also build more houses.

"Please don't misunderstand," Rosalynn Carter has said, "this is NOT charity. It is NOT a giveaway. Each family must qualify for an interest-free loan from Habitat which they'll pay back over the next 20 years while their payments go into a revolving fund to provide homes for other families. They must pay a modest down payment. They must put in many hours of volunteer services helping other families in need. And then they go to work on their own home-building crew!"

There are fewer criteria to be a Habitat volunteer than a Habitat homebuyer, activists say. People can volunteer time, materials, labor, help with the group's administration, or make tax-deductible contributions or no-interest loans.

If the organization's needs seem great, it's because they are, Hettiger says.

"We have a very ripe market here in Peoria for low-cost housing," he says. "A lot of people need it. We can't even begin to cope with it. All we can do is make a little dent in it. That's all we can accomplish."

Such accomplishments are significant, and widespread. Besides Peoria, West-Central Illinois boasts established and newly formed Habitat chapters in Galesburg, Bloomington and Springfield. Much of their good work has continued from last summer, when the worldwide group celebrated its 15th anniversary by building 1,500 homes in 16 weeks in 225 communities throughout North America. There are rewards, Hettiger says, nodding.

"The great sense of participation is because they do see something happening," Ray says. "I mentioned the 200 people that worked on this one house a while back. We put 2,000 man-hours in this real old house (to) bring it up to date and everything. We worked all winter on that-- had people down there three times a week in the winter

Ray Hettiger at Habitat For Humanity's Peoria office.

months, and they just were thrilled with the idea that they were taking an old house that could have been demolished, restoring it, and then having a family taking it over. So, yeah, there's a real sense of accomplishment."

That sense is bolstered by another positive sense, he says, like when the new homeowners pitch in. And move in.

"As you might expect, they're generally very thrilled because they're coming from a low-cost public housing-- which isn't the best of environments, to say the least. What's interesting is that most of the people who come into our housing are buying a house and getting equity in it for less than they paid for public housing. So there's a great sense of pride on their part and, of course, every one of them has to put in 250 man-hours of work on the house while it's under construction. So they feel that sense of being part of building a new house or rehabbing an old one.

"When they move in, they're all excited, just ready to go-- and we stay with them, go back on a regular basis, work with them if they have problems. Eventually, through their own efforts, they become part of the organization; they come back and work on other houses. So there's a sense of enthusiasm, a little bit. That's what keeps us rolling."

Welfare unattractive, family trapped

(PEORIA)-- Plastic tacked and taped onto the windows billows with the blowing wind. Inside, Wilma and Len sit on an old couch and talk about welfare.

"It's tough," he says. "There's not very many jobs and the ones there don't pay much. I've been up to Kewanee, down to Pekin. It's the same all over.

"I don't know," he adds. "Seems like it's getting worse."

Len and Wilma are two of about six million Americans who the federal government calls "unemployables." No longer even included in unemployment statistics, they're people who'd accept work, but no longer actively seek jobs; mothers who receive Aid to Families with Dependent Children (AFDC); or others the government dismisses in a classification: "discouraged."

Len is discouraged, he says.

"Nothing to do," says Len, sitting with his beefy arms folded across his chest. "May as well kill a little time."

More than a little effort is going into overhauling welfare. From conservatives to liberals, there's some support for some type of change. But the type and the consequences-- on both recipients and taxpayers-- remains unclear.

Welfare is a broad term covering 59 federally assisted plans from local, state and federal agencies. The assistance to the poor includes AFDC, unemployment compensation, medical assistance, and township relief.

Len and Wilma-- a reasonably healthy white couple in their early 40s with limited education-- receive a monthly welfare check for about $500 from the Illinois Department of Public Aid, plus other benefits. Some may regard that as generous, but it's less than previous years in real dollars. Since 1970, benefit increases have trailed so far behind inflation that the real value of AFDC has fallen more than 33 percent, the U.S. Department of Labor reports.

Even at it comparably low level, welfare keeps Len and Wilma and their two sons going. But if Len took a low-paying job-- the most common type available-- his family would lose money, he says. Trading some of their benefits for a low wage won't even lift Len up to the poverty level-- about $13,000 for a family of four.

"I try a little, but I don't expect much," says Len, leaning back and bringing a hand across his balding head. Married for almost 20 years, Wilma and Len have lived in Peoria since the early '80s, when they moved here from Missouri. There, Len worked in a warehouse; here, he formerly worked at an area cleaners.

"I loaded washers," he says, glancing absently around the room. "I worked in a big steam room. It always seemed so cool outside after standing in that heat so long."

He was one of several who were laid off, and he exhausted his unemployment insurance. Now he-- and his family-- depend on welfare.

Wilma remembers that she used to want to be a nurse's aide. Now she's content being a homemaker, she says.

"We keep each other on the ball," she says with a smile, slapping Len's leg. He reaches out and strokes her long, straight brown hair, pulled back in a pony tail.

The couple now rents a white frame house up the bluff from downtown after their previous residence was sold.

"It was a real mess here when we moved in," he says. "We fixed it up."

The sofa fills half of their tidy living room, which also has one chair, an end table, an occasional table and a faded braided rug. And old 8-track tape player sits on an older console television set next to a videocassette recorder and library videotapes.

A more worn green rug is spread beneath the dining-room table, which is covered by a vinyl tablecloth. Beyond is a clean kitchen. A small adjacent bedroom contains a bed with a "Happy Days" sticker on the footboard.

•

Lawmakers have been discussing various welfare reform packages for years. Whether in the House or Senate, the federal or state levels, the thrust of most efforts seems to be to encourage recipients to leave the dole, to convert welfare to a short-term program.

"Welfare is an income-maintenance program," said

President Clinton, who began working on welfare reform when he was chairman of the National Governors Association more than five years ago.

"It ought to be a training and work program with an income support component.

"(Welfare reform) would force people to work if jobs can be found," Clinton continued. "If they won't, they would lose that portion of the assistance."

Such reforms could provide initiative and create productive citizens independent of government handouts, Clinton said.

However, Bradley University economist Kal Goldberg says incentives alone won't work.

"The problem with incentives is that many workers displaced from manufacturers that have suffered downturns are older, and even with retraining they have a hard time being attractive to potential employers," He said. "And younger people have to find employment in less-skilled, lower-paying jobs. So older people have to make do and survive hand-to-mouth, and younger people have to lower their expectations."

Other reform ideas range from "workfare" (where recipients must labor on public works such as roads or parks) and cash grants for schooling to welfare "contracts" (reciprocal agreements pledging certain performances to remain eligible for benefits) and establishing a national minimum standard of living.

Len runs his hand over his head again; he takes a deep breath.

"Sometimes there's a job in the ads," he says. "I saw one once and was going to call the next morning-- because I was working on the car-- but the ad wasn't there the next day."

"I'm a pretty fair mechanic," he says, brightening a bit. "I had a Pinto for awhile, kept it up, and I've worked on Fords, Dodges. I had a Dodge Charger a while back. Boy, that car'd really burn rubber!

"(But) there's no mechanic work, either," he says, shrugging. "Reading the paper is about all I can do."

Near a discarded newspaper on the floor lies a half-finished jigsaw puzzle. On the table, a puzzle lies finished except for one missing piece.

"I got a Rubik's Cube," Len says. "I never have figured that out. I don't have the patience for puzzles."

Activities center around their home and family, he says.

"We don't do much, really," he says. "When we get a notion, we'll go on a walk."

When he was working, they occasionally took short trips, Len recalls.

"I remember down in Clarksville, Mo., they had a big old lift you could go up in," he says. "I didn't like that much-- just sitting up there, hanging by a thread, waiting to be moved. No, sir."

Their children-- a boy in grade school, another in high school-- are shy. The older one smiles a lot; the younger runs a lot.

"He can't sit still," Len says, shaking his head. "He's always wound up-- keeps you going all day."

Children are the forgotten victims of welfare, says Goldberg.

"Programs for parents just aren't being attended to," he says. "And in the long run, the needs of children are not being attended to. The country's throwing away a whole generation. It's a human tragedy."

Wilma and Len's teen-ager collects aluminum cans to redeem for cash. He uses the money for treats, he says. One afternoon--in the shadows of downtown banks, the Peoria County Courthouse, and Caterpillar's world head-quarters, the boy went through four trash cans at the Main Street intersection.

"It's better on a day after the pushcarts are here," he said. •

Wilma has a less conspicuous procedure to acquire the family's welfare check, but she and Len still feel uncom-fortable. They don't like the label welfare-- the word itself. Len sends Wilma inside the currency exchange to get the check while he waits in the car with their boys.

"We pick it up, go to the bank, pay bills, and go home," he says. "It takes an hour a month."

A line of mostly women forms outside the exchange a few blocks from downtown Peoria. Some of the women have children; many are alone. There are no couples. Few talk.

After the doors are unlocked at 9 a.m., dozens of people patiently stand in four lines. On the wall are posted signs about food stamps and free income tax help. After several minutes, a little chatter and civil conversation starts between strangers waiting with each other.

At the teller's window, Wilma presents her plastic identification card and an authorization for the check. She shows neither relief nor dread as she turns and pockets the check and walks out.

Silently, she slides into the car's front seat. She and Len put on their seat belts and the family drives out of the emptying parking lot.

•

Welfare draws criticism like stink draws bugs. Officials complain that it's a bureaucracy that traps the poor, it breaks up families, it encourages idleness, it creates self-perpetuating dependency.

Len agrees.

But he tempers his own frustrations with a question.

"Some people get mad because they think welfare makes poverty worse," he says. "I don't know. You can't think a clutch went out just because you tried to fix it."

Election aftermath:
No salvation, but hope

(EAST PEORIA)-- Rain runs down my windshield as I drive home from reporting on Election 1992. It won't let up; it's been a long night, when flowery flakes of snow weren't the only signs of a storm. A flood of hopelessness also flowed out from polling booths. Away.

Certainly, George Bush was defeated. Possibly, Bill Clinton was mandated to change the course of the country.

I motored through slush and shivered and smiled.

... time blurs.

●

I was about nine years old, and a tornado warning had my family huddled in the dim flashlight glow of a damp basement, listening to winds howl and pound the house. My younger brother... panicked. Instinctively-- unaware why or how, really-- I... calmed him. We read and talked and touched; we were grounded to each other right there-- despite the twister outside. Distracted.

Afterward, when I realized the danger and devastation nearby, I shuddered. A close call.

●

Now, there's a calming distraction in America: a new leader.

Clinton offers hope, not salvation. He seems somewhat progressive. And practical. He didn't promise the impossible-- a GOP fantasy of cutting taxes AND the deficit. Clinton seems more mindful of people's needs, and... merciful toward the middle class and the poor; the elderly and minorities; the environment and women and others rejected by recent Republicans.

Clinton HAS character, enduring months of questions-- outrageous and honest. And he has Al Gore.

But Bush has... his conservative dogma, that thought that any government should do less, and the best government should do nothing-- unless it benefits the rich with tax breaks. Bush-- and Reagan-- preferred the private sector. But Bush-- not even always consistent or sincere-sounding-- didn't fool Americans for long.

Voters knew corporations handle human affairs only if they're profitable, leaving everything else to people and our government. We choose representatives to help ourselves: education, infrastructure and opportunity; taking care of old people and the needy; protecting our borders and the environment. Who wants the EPA run by businessmen like GM's?

And who wants public affairs like family leave run by business? We have no say there, in the private sector. The public sector is ours, is US.

So voters defeated the de-regulators and an administration dismantling the federal judiciary, especially the Supreme Court. The electorate rejected 12 years of increasing intolerance and supply-side bankers.

The road splashes. Again, time blurs.

•

It's 1896, and William Jennings Bryan was speaking in Springfield, campaigning for president. "I stand with Jefferson," he said. "The banks must go out of the governing business. We will win over the idle holders of idle capital. We will not legislate to make the rich prosperous and hope that prosperity will leak down to those below."

Now, doing something similar won't be simple. There's the rumored banking crisis, and the $4 trillion debt legacy of the failed Reagan-Bush economics.

As the wipers slap the glass, I know it's not too soon to act. After all, if the deficit, joblessness and the health care problem are too much, hopes will fade. The result could be a right-wing reaction dwarfing the Reagan "Revolution," a backlash blaming "liberals."

So, progressives must pressure the promising President-elect.

I arrive home at 3 a.m., eager for dawn.

Author at Cubs' Arizona camp. (Photo courtesy of Greg Wagner.)

Personal ▬▬▬▬▬▬▬▬▬

> *War correspondent Ernie Pyle in 1943 wrote, "I write from the worm's-eye point of view."*
>
> **--Press Cuttings**

I'm no worm, but I try to stay grounded. Elsewhere, I write about the year's flood, but I admit the disaster hit me hardest when I saw scrapbooks and yearbooks, clippings and belongings marking my life floating in my basement. Trying to save the mildewing mess, I found parts of my past: years and careers, attitudes and change. I guess essays like these are also bits of a background: first-person and personal points of view that remember a relative or an experience, express a thought or an opinion, give some perspective or a slant to something that's extraordinary, like catching a Hall of Famer's fly ball, or ordinary, like praying about a dog.

Out of my field of dreams

(MESA, Arizona)-- On the first day of baseball camp, everyone knew who I was. I was the guy who'd been shot in the head by a line drive off the bat of Jim Gasparo, a California Cub fan built like the Incredible Hulk.

"In 18 years in the majors, I never saw a ball bounce off a guy's head like like," said an amazed Jimmy Piersall. "When it happened, I called for the paramedics."

Piersall's baseball career was chronicled in the campy film *Fear Strikes Out* , cablecast the night before I came here to Randy Hundley's Baseball Camp, where I became the first injury.

By week's end, Piersall and 10 other ex-big leaguers saw about a third of the 53 campers coping with stiff arms and legs, pulled or torn muscles and reality kicking dirt in the faces of their fantasies. And through all of the discomfort, effort and competition, there wasn't one complaint. Just joy, and fun.

Fun wasn't immediately evident on the pitcher's mound that first day, when I lay dazed, sprawled in the dirt like a pile of soiled laundry. After impact, I'd quickly sat up to see if I could still throw out the runner, but the ball was about 50 feet away, near our dugout. And instead of a medic, the trainer from the San Francisco Giants and ex-Cub Jose Cardenal ran to me. The trainer shoved me down, put a bag of ice on my forehead, and asked how many fingers he held up.

"Uh, two," I said, stammering as I noticed my blood trickling down my face.

"Hey, you right!" said Cardenal, who leaned over and shaded the sun, asking, "You hokay, mon? Hey, am I black or white?"

"I'm not sure," I coughed. "You're Cuban."

After being helped to the bleachers, I watched our team-- managed by ex-journeyman catcher/first baseman Gene Oliver-- beat up on the squad managed by Cardenal and Piersall.

The mid-January camp's former major league ballplayers included several veterans from the 1969 Cubs lineup: Billy Williams, Ron Santo, Glenn Beckert, Jim Hickman, Hank Aguirre, Oliver and Hundley. Besides Piersall and Cardenal, two other surprises were Hall of Famer Hoyt Wilhelm, who had the 1970 Cubs season on his record, and fellow pitcher Burt Hooten, with a 1972 Cubs no-hitter to his credit.

The average age of the pros was 50; my team averaged 40. One of six teams created in a pre-camp draft, we included Joe Kosala, a husky Chicago cop who moonlights as a first baseman and a film actor (*The Fugitive, Above The Law, Code of Silence*); Louie Ruffolo, a slender Wheaton Italian who played like a Natural; George Goodall, a Belleville retiree and second baseman who still smacks the ball like when he played with Joe Garigiola decades ago; Finny Aronson, a radiologist/outfielder and compact dynamo who hit in the clutch despite a hand injury; Ron Cowell, a Palatine businessman with the legs of a 90-year-old cowboy but a heart like Ernie Banks'; Tom Luebke, a Naperville contractor with an easy smile and hard instincts that kept him healthy enough to pitch against the major leaguers; Rick Ulbrich, a Barrington financier/infielder with hands like baskets and knees like ballpark franks; Stan Banyon, an Indianapolis catcher with the temperment of a serial killer; and me, an outfielder/first baseman who left my pitching experience back at college, where I picked up journalism.

"You don't have to be a super athlete to play in our camps," Hundley said. "If you're 30 or older, we want you on the roster."

Most of the campers were first-time "rookies" like me. But more than a few were returning, like Banyon. A handful could be called veterans, like Goodall, who'd been to more than a dozen camps.

"Some people might think I'm nuts," Goodall said. "But to do this at my age is one of the most enjoyable experiences of my life."

Other campers included Dan Sullivan, the retired owner of the San Antonio minor-league franchise where Santo and Williams first played, and T.C. Coulter, a Baby Boomer who exhibited the most painful running of anyone all week. He'd sprint toward first like he needed an aluminum walker. He audibly groaned when he headed toward a batted ball: "Eeenh," he'd squeal. "Eeenh."

Peoria standup comic/designated hitter Royce Elliott and shortstop David Rudstein and catcher Trip Demaree all were great guys and decent players. My roommate was Bob Smith, a Joliet Caterpillar worker who ended up as Santo's team's leftfielder. My clubhouse locker was between Tom Klingaman, an Indianapolis salesman who tore a bicep on Day 2, and Hilhelm, who up close looks a lot like Bob Newhart.

"How ya' doin', Gorby?" Wilhelm greeted me each morning after Williams nicknamed me and my bruised forehead after the ex-Soviet premier. Through most of the week, the heavy-lidded Wilhelm was deadpan, but a smirk occasionally crossed his face. At Harry and Steve's sports bar near the hotel, campers and big-leaguers gathered nightly to watch videos of the day's games. One night, in what passed for a tender moment here, Oliver leaned over and kissed a woman's cheek. Wilhelm, who's also a Florida farmer, looked up from his beer, looked around, and, to no one in particular, asked, "Whassat? Sounded like a cow pullin' its leg outta the mud."

Besides seven nights in the first-class Ramada Renaissance, the Hundley Baseball Camp package included a regulation Cubs uniform, breakfast and lunch daily, a baseball with all of the big leaguers' autographs, both planned and spontaneous memorabilia, an awards banquet, a personalized Lousiville Slugger bat, a video of the Big Game against the pros, various photographs and genuine camaraderie among campers and with the big leaguers.

Whether reminiscing about their own careers in the dugout tunnel or lounging by the pool, the big leaguers remained accessible and friendly from early morning to late night. And their attitudes remained good-natured and unflappable.

One morning after a camper brought in three, one-dozen boxes of baseballs for Hooten to sign, the former knuckle-curve pitcher looked up from his locker-room chair and smiled weakly.

"For all this, you shoulda at least brought in some doughnuts."

The daily routine begins in the hotel restaurant with campers pounding down coffee and various ballplayer remedies for hangovers. ("We want this to be as close to a major-league experience as we can make it," Hundley announced at the opening meeting. "So just like the majors, you guys will have a curfew. Only here, no one's allowed in BEFORE a 1 a.m.") after a bus ride to Hohokam Stadium-- the Cubs' spring training home, where we first used its renovated clubhouse-- we donned our big-league uniforms. (In fact, we were also the first to wear the Cubs' new design, which brought back buttons and belts.) Then we were transported to Fitch Park, the Cubs' minor-league complex where, on three diamonds, players were led through stretching exercises before rotating from outfield drills and batting cage instruction to infield drills and shagging flies.

"The 14 years I spent as a major league baseball player have enabled me to authentically recreate not only spring training, but also that special feeling of being a big leaguer," Hundley said.

Alone or in pairs, the big leaguers spent mornings offering one-on-one tips in fundamentals most guys hadn't used in years-- but never exactly forgot, either. The pros spent afternoons directing their teams in a week-long tournament for the privilege of starting in Saturday's Big Game. The intra-squad games recognized that campers couldn't pitch all week (or at all), so we batted against the pitching machines, all called Iron Mike.

Bemoaning his team's third consecutive loss on Wednesday, Hickman shook his head and sighed, "I can't believe my guys got shut out by a robot!"

After the games and a shuttle back to the showers-- and before late afternoons of hot tubs and backrubs-- there were lessons in the ruthless locker-room humor refined over long careers in the bigs.

On Tuesday-- the 74th anniversary of the Wrigley family buying into the Cubs for $50,000-- Oliver reviewed the second day's games.

"... and Knight went five for five at the plate, coming back from a serious head injury," he said. "He took Hoyt Wilhelm at his word when Hoyt said, 'Use your head, Billy'."

Non-stop ribbing came from big-leaguers and campers alike. On Wednesday of that week, Santo got word he'd been hired as the Cubs' new color commentator for radio broadcasts, and his team immediately made ticket requests for the coming season.

In the midst of analyzing a game, Piersall stopped and sneered: "Y'know, I think of all the years it took for me to get to the big leagues, and I sit here and see you guys dressed in these uniforms and I want to puke."

The spring training dream and big-league illusion was achieved in individual ways, and the male-bonding along the way was harmlessly unrelenting and thankfully juvenile.

Recovered just enough to dress in uniform, limp to first base and bat with a pinch runner, Kosala on Friday stood at his locker in his jersey and jockstrap, exposing his injury-- a black-and-white backside bruise that literally streaked from his hip to his ankle.

He cursed Piersall.

"Hey, Jimmy, see what happens when you try to teach guys fielding grounders and hook slides at the same time?"

Piersall shrugged apologetically and offered to sign anything Kosala wanted. Their eyes met and Kosala leaned over.

Piersall took a felt marker and autographed the back of Kosala's thigh. A day later at the awards banquet, Kosala whispered with some concern that the autograph didn't wash off.

"He got me again," he hissed with a grin.

Kosala's return to our lineup helped us become the first Hundley camp team to ever go undefeated, our 5-0 record bolstered by an error-free outfield, solid hitting and a team chemistry mixing a sober approach and a silly sense of humor. So we won the right to start against the big leaguers at Saturday's Big Game at Hohokam.

That morning, psyching up players and campers alike, the 6-foot-4 Aguirre pulled his cap low over his eyes, leaned forward on a table, and puffed on a cigarette.

"Remember this 'life-time fantasy'," he said in a raspy voice, " 'cause today, you're dead."

Indeed. Campers were allowed to bat through their squad lineups each inning, but the big leaguers just got three outs. That was plenty. While weaker hitters looked at lobs from Aguirre or Wilhelm or Hooten, those of us batting decently saw smoke and heat and breaking balls only visible by watching their vapor trails. The pros won, 22-12, but there were still memorable moments.

In the first inning of the Big Game-- as I fought outfield stage fright-- Billy Williams hit a towering fly ball in my direction. Behind the plate, the metal stands shining through the small crowd made it difficult to see the ball coming off the bat. But I recovered enough to pick it up, run toward the fence and foul line, and catch it.

And I kept it, later taking it to Williams, who gave me another Hall of Fame autograph.

All of the souvenirs still sparkle, but don't overshadow the warm memories a camper keeps-- like the other demonstration of my "grace."

On Wednesday, when we were trying to finish a game against Beckert's team during a rare afternoon rain, a lazy pop fly was hit to me in the outfield. I jogged into position, but as I pulled up, my feet left the wet grass and I landed flat on my back.

My eyes still on the ball, I realized I wouldn't be able to regain my footing, so I lunged sideways, lying down.

I caught the ball.

As I got to my feet and threw the ball to Goodall at second, I could see Beckert throwing batting helmets around his dugout, shaking his head and shouting, "What has to happen to beat these guys?"

'Ethical investor'-- oxymoron?

(MACOMB)-- Hello. My name is Bill Knight. I'm a... capitalist.

I'm not addicted to "smoking stock," or anything. But the new attractions and illusions of owning minute pieces of corporate America had me concerned enough to contrive a sort of 12-step program to better cope with... shareholder anxiety. With "stock guilt."

About 20 years ago, I was one of hundreds of thousands of American college kids who thought we knew everything. One thing was that capitalism was stupid, if not evil. I tied the market system to imperialism, colonialism, racism and just about every negative "ism" short of... well, alcoholism.

I'm still not wild about it. But as I read more about capitalism, I realized its ideal form at least offered opportunities not available in other existing economic systems. After all, there was a certain, symmetrical tidiness to some individuals pooling their resources to help promote progress-- not profits, but growth. However, historically, business run amok led to robber barons and the exploitation of consumers and workers. Such economic injustices and the resulting unfair distribution of wealth caused some to get government to try to control capital. Things like the Sherman Anti-Trust Act and the Federal Reserve Board were well-intentioned, but they really failed, instead permitting a new and increasingly powerful corporate structure to control government.

Free enterprise isn't. Capital controls most natural and financial resources, and the products and services created from them. Sobering, huh?

When I left a newspaper job with a chunk of retirement change, I had to use it or lose it. (Did Adam Smith say that?) I juggled the internal conflict by opting for a program called socially responsible, or ethical, investing. That, too, is maybe an illusion, but a comforting one, providing for screens guarding against securities from polluters, union-busters, arms merchants, vivisectionists, racists, sexists and so on, and screens seeking out stocks and bonds from progressive outfits, from Ben & Jerry's Ice Cream to Apple computers. Such schemes sell well, according to the Social Investment Forum, a 1,000-member association that says $650 billion in such investments now exist.

Promoters claim SRI "empowers investors to use their resources to promote corporate responsibility," but it actually seems more like swapping baseball cards with buddies. Such investments can reflect your ideals, but mostly-- in physicians' terms-- ethical investing will "do no harm."

Socially responsible investing would genuinely be effective if it somehow reallocated capital from anti-social to social missions-- from guns to butter or environmental degradation to stewardship, as Mark Dowie has said in *The Nation* magazine. My holdings (Geez, is this a "portfolio"?) don't. But they promise me access to annual reports and stockholders' meetings, where gadfly groups like the Interfaith Center on Corporate Responsibility crash capital's party and raise Cain.

So, I've read the "Guide To Understanding Money & Markets," the *Wall Street Journal's* incomprehensible but graphically appealing brochure that I suspect prepares me for similarly useless annual reports. I've begun to acknowledge stock market pages in newspaper agate, scrolls on TV and broker remotes on radio. And I've examined my stock: U S West (a "responsible" communications company), Woolworth (an "ethical" company), and-- wait a sec'-- Carnival Cruises? (Hey! Get my broker on the line!)

Time waits for no one

(QUINCY)-- The business of America is busy-ness.

My grandfather was busy. For decades he labored for Standard Oil, first running a successful Moberly, Mo., gas station, then driving and selling throughout central Illinois, winning prizes and logging miles.

And time.

More than 25 years ago he was here, sitting at his backyard picnic table behind his white ranch house in a subdivision east of town. Looking up at the stars one night, spending some vacation time with my brother and me, he sighed and smiled and said, "Billy, I can do a year's work in 11 months, but not in 12."

Then, I thought that was harmless doubletalk from a tired old guy. Now, I know he was onto something.

Today, Americans work a month more a year than they did then, according to a study by Laura Leete-Guy of Case Western Reserve University and Juliet Schor of Harvard.

"America is starved for time," concludes the study, entitled "The Great American Time Squeeze: Trends in Work and Leisure, 1969-89."

"Increasing numbers of people are finding themselves overworked, stressed out and heavily taxed by the joint demands of work and family life," it adds.

"When surveyed, Americans report that they have only 16 hours a week (left) after the obligations of job and household are taken care of," Schor told *Z* magazine. "Thirty percent of adults say that they experience high stress nearly every day; even higher numbers report high stress once or twice a week. Half the population now says they have too little time for their families."

Co-author Leete-Guy added that, "Americans who have all the work they want are now working and commuting 158 more hours a year-- in effect, adding a 13th month of work since 1969. The number of paid days off dropped in the 1980s."

Paid time off-- vacations, holidays sick leave and personal days-- decreased about 15 percent in the 1980s alone, shows the study, which also pointed out that Americans' working hours are now at about the same level they were during World War II.

Indeed, the average American puts in a 40-hour week, gets 11 official holidays and 12 days paid vacation-- all after five years on the job, according to the Bureau of Labor Statistics. In other countries, workers do better:

· The Japanese work 42 hours a week, but they average 16 days of paid vacation and a whopping 20 holidays;

· The British work 39-hour weeks, and get eight holidays and 25 days of vacation yearly;

· The Germans work a 38-hour week, get 10 holidays and 30 days of paid vacation.

Schor-- who also wrote the book *The Overworked American*, which was published in paperback this year-- observes that the trend results from a few factors. First, workers feel they must supplement their incomes to keep up with increasing costs for health care and housing. Next, some employers feel that over-working employees with overtime hours avoids paying additional workers' benefits-- and few complain. After all, if the only jobs available work people to frazzles, it's better than not working. Finally, some employers feel they have to get more work for the same wage-- essentially cutting payrolls.

"The game of lowering wages can get insidious," Schor

Author's grandpa, A.A. Knight (right), spends time selling for the Standard Oil Co. more than 50 years ago.

wrote. "Once the highest in the world, U.S. manufacturing wages have fallen substantially for a decade and now rank below many West European nations.

"How far should (wages) go?" she continued. "Korea, Brazil and India are growing competitors. If corporations demand a decline to the poverty wages in many countries, should American workers simply accede?"

Many Americans oddly also suffer from unemployment or involuntary part-time work or work for temporary agencies, which usually pay no fringe benefits, Schor added.

"One of the great ironies of our present situation," she wrote, "is that overwork for the majority has been accompanied by the growth of enforced idleness for the minority. The proportion of the labor force who cannot work as many hours as they would like has more than doubled in the last 20 years. Just as surely as our economic system is 'underproducing' leisure for some, it is 'overproducing' it for others."

For all of the extra time and effort, what do the overworked get?

Not money.

Real wages have fallen since 1973, according to the AFL-CIO's Department of Economic Research, which also found that U.S. factory workers earn lower wage rates than their European counterparts. Germans, for example, earn an average of $21.30 an hour.

And for all of the extra effort, what do we get?

Not time.

I'd love to have that long-gone time with my grandfather again. Most hard-working people are torn between obligations of making a living, and living. No one should have to sacrifice their time with each other to survive in the U.S. economy.

(*The Great American Time Squeeze* is available from Public Interest Publications, P.O. Box 229, Arlington, VA 22210. The cost is $5, plus $3 shipping and handling.)

Doctor is in

(PEORIA)-- "May I help?" the receptionist greeted me when she answered. I mumbled, and she replied, "Sorry. Doctor has moved to Pittsburgh."

I convulsed.

The earpiece of the phone seemed to throb against my temple, swollen along with about half of my head. My skull looked like a Neanderthal's, and I wondered why medical assistants rarely say, "THE doctor."

Tired and wired after about six hours sleep in the last four nights, I felt barbaric. I had a temperature of 102 degrees, a cheek so puffy my mouth wouldn't open far enough to eat anything thicker than a wheat thin, and no desire to chew food more demanding than apple sauce, or attend to anything.

No longer willing-- or able-- to "bite the bullet," I'd taken a deep breath ("Arghh!") and called my dentist, who'd left town.

Tooth pain is unique. When something goes wrong inside your mouth, it's almost as if there's some pulsating, prehistoric organ demanding to be surgically removed

Personal

from your otherwise-evolved, modern body.

But it's really unlike anything.

A cavity or an abcess or an impacted tooth isn't like when you stub your toe or break your leg or scrape your elbow or jam your thumb. Then and there, you can clutch it or hold it, rub it or even, yes, put it in your mouth.

What can you do with tooth pain?

Suffer.

One-celled animals don't know how lucky they are.

Dental hygiene for me is brushing, flossing and rinsing. On this occasion, I added groaning, lying in a fetal position and letting tears fill one eye.

En route to an emergency visit to another dentist who I've never seen, pain persists, supplemented by a little panic.

The doctor's diagnosis (Oops, sorry: "DOCTOR'S diagnosis") is one of my wisdom teeth ran roughshod over a molar, trapped some food somewhere, allowed decay to set it and infected my face. This ugly situation requires that the wisdom tooth be extracted and the abcessed infection released and relieved.

Resigned, sitting in the chair and sighing ("Ow!"), I get prepped. First, some red gel is daubed on the area with a swab. (It's supposed to taste sweet and numb the gum, but excess drips out of my contorted mouth with all of the flavor of aluminum bubble gum.) Next, a face/nose mask pumps gas into my lungs and brain. (It's supposed to relax me and it works: I drift off slightly, thinking how this stuff might've made a fun weekend during college.) Lastly, a novocaine-filled needle jabs in and deadens a handful of spots inside my mouth (and what seems like the outside of my body from my scalp to my chest).

The dentist is apparently sympathetic. This might be care for his fellow man or concern that a patient in pain may not pay promptly, but it doesn't matter. He gives me a Walkman to help distract me. While he gathers his instruments I absently fiddle with the dial and settle on a local radio station. During the hour-long procedure I hear Manfred Mann's "Doo Wah Diddy" and Al Jarreau's "Moonlighting" and wonder whether I'll henceforth associate the songs with pain.

I've always tried to be a good patient: I hold whimpering to a minimum. Considering most of this stranger's gloved hands seem to be filling my head, I feel pretty cooperative. I submit to the routine terror and torture ("Just get it over with," I think).

Some medieval-looking metal tool passes past my eyes, enters my mouth and grabs something way back there. The dentist moves his whole upper body side to side, pulls slightly and finally rocks something out of a socket.

I squint, wince, flinch and gasp when my jawbone audibly cracks.

Surrounding an adjacent molar is a rubber guard no bigger than a golf green. In front of a bright light hovering above us like a tiny UFO, two masked faces peer directly at my eyes. They leave my field of vision.

I'm reclining so steeply, my feet awkwardly stick up in the air from the chair.

The mask on my nose keeps pumping, the hose shoved beneath my tongue keeps sucking, the drill and its water keep whirling.

There's a new pinch and a flash of pain.

I convulse.

"Comfortable?" someone asks.

I grunt and think like some primitive: "Doctor help Bill now?"

It's a dog's life

The air is as hot and thick as oatmeal; nights are uncomfortable. With a sinister indifference, the ground fog disrupts mornings. The sun-- when the clouds infrequently break up-- is baking the mid-day ground, making the soil the earth's **"crust."**

But it's not the heat, it's the HUMIDITY, here in the Dog Days of an unforgettable Illinois summer.

"Dog Days"? How did DOGS end up saddled as a species with sweltering misery? Despite the honor of guarding Plato's Republic and founding Rome (no, the famous Capitoline Wolf was NOT a wolf), the cliche might stem from dogs' consistently lowly station in the Bible. There, they're downgraded; look it up.

Secular literature at least seems to offer a more personal portrait of "man's best friend," to which I'm glad to add my own testimony.

When I was a preschooler, I readied for bed with the standard but rather gruesome childhood prayer ("Now I lay me down to sleep/ I pray the Lord my soul to keep./ If I should die before I wake/ I pray the Lord my soul to take"). I always added some afterthoughts, including a regular request about protection from tornadoes. But this kid felt such a kinship with our family dog, Duke, that I also had a special plea that if, indeed, I DID die before I awoke, I hoped it'd somehow be with Duke. And as long as we were both dying, I prayed that we should be laid to rest together. To me, that seemed to be a perfectly natural petition to God.

But-- after 15 years-- Duke died first.

Now I find that English poet Alexander Pope preceded me by a few hundred years, writing, "... admitted to that equal sky, his faithful dog shall bear him company."

From such masters to moderns such as John Updike, other writers express wonderful thoughts on these creatures:

Lord Byron: "The poor dog, in life the firmest friend,
"The first to welcome, the foremost to defend."

Elizabeth Barrett Browning: "Therefore to this dog will I,
"Tenderly not scornfully,
"Render praise and favor."

Sir Walter Scott: "Recollect that the Almighty, who gave the dog to be companion of our pleasures and our toils, hath invested him with a nature noble and incapable of deceit."

•

A late friend of mine put it shorter, if not better, about my own late 14-year buddy, Beefheart: "He never lies, and he always forgives." I hope they're together now.

But the best came from Vest-- U.S. Sen. George Graham Vest, who in 1884 summed it up in a speech in the nation's Capitol:

"The one absolutely unselfish friend that man can have in this selfish world, the one that never deserts him, the one that never proves ungrateful or treacherous, is his dog. A man's dog stands by him in prosperity and in poverty, in health and in sickness. He will sleep on the cold ground, where the wintry winds blow and the snow drives fiercely, if only he may be near his master's side. He will kiss the hand that has no food to offer; he will lick the wounds and sores that come in encounter with the roughness of the world. He guards the sleep of his pauper master as if he were a prince. When all other friends desert, he remains. When riches take wing and reputation falls to pieces, he is as constant in his love as the sun in its journey through the heavens."

Ah, the sun.

The heat.

"The more I see of men," said 18th century French Revolutionary Jean Roland, "the better I like dogs."

Yeah, it's NOT the heat, it's the HUMANITY.

Every dog has its day.

Forgive and forget?

(PEORIA)-- "Forgive and forget," the cliche goes. But perhaps this observation-- or advice-- is seamless, insepa-rable.

For example, my wife's 95-year-old aunt doesn't dispute

a Peoria department store's right to evict her lunch-hour bridge club from the store's tea room more than 40 years ago. But in the mere act of remembering it-- and repeating it-- she reveals her regret and disappointment.

Is it any wonder-- for those who still wonder-- why a recurring rage remains felt by peoples whose histories include persecution?

Forgiveness may not be possible without forgetting, and forgetting (or forgetfulness) is difficult, if not impossible, when a crime against humanity is the memory.

· Native Americans have a life expectancy of about 44 years, with the highest infant mortality rate on the continent and epidemics of diseases otherwise managed elsewhere.

· By the time of the Emancipation Proclamation, millions of black Africans had been kidnapped and forcibly made "African Americans." Since it began as a source for cheap labor in 1619, slavery scarred the western hemisphere. The scars remain.

· A more recent genocide was perpetrated against Jews, who suffered a Holocaust as part of centuries of discrimination. And in today's headlines are victims of famine and greed in Somalia and Brazil, in Cambodia and Croatia.

Unforgettable pain and suffering. Unforgiveable acts of treachery and shame.

To err is human, goes another cliche. Forgiveness? Divine. For most of us mere mortals, the best we can hope for is perspective. It's unrealistic and maybe unreasonable to expect descendants of slaves, of residents of reservations or concentration camps, or even of exploited women or workers to absolutely forget.

And as British author D. H. Lawrence said of the Native American: "He doesn't believe in us and our civilization... we push him off the face of the earth. He is dispossessed of life, and unforgiving."

Mayfly Productions